MINI SAGAS

Fictional Fun

OXFORDSHIRE & THE SOUTH OF ENGLAND

EDITED BY HELEN DAVIES

First published in Great Britain in 2011 by:

 Young**Writers**

Remus House
Coltsfoot Drive
Peterborough
PE2 9BF
Telephone: 01733 890066
Website: www.youngwriters.co.uk

FOREWORD

Young Writers was established in 1990 with the aim of encouraging and nurturing writing skills in young people and giving them the opportunity to see their work in print. By helping them to become more confident and expand their creative skills, we hope our young writers will be encouraged to keep writing as they grow.

School pupils nationwide have been exercising their minds to create their very own short stories, Mini Sagas, using no more than fifty words, to be included here in our latest competition, *The Adventure Starts Here* ...

The entries we received showed an impressive level of creativity and imagination, providing an absorbing look into the eager minds of our future authors.

YE CONTENTS OF AUTHORS

Congratulations to all young writers who appear in this book

Chilton Primary School, Chilton

Compass Point: South Street School, Bedminster

Greatworth Primary School, Banbury

Katesgrove Primary School, Reading

Kingham Primary School, Chipping Norton

Kirtlington Primary School, Kirtlington

Pensford Primary School, Pensford

St John's RC Primary School, Banbury

Wetherby School, Notting Hill

Wolvercote Primary School, Wolvercote

MINI⚡SAGAS

SPACE ADVENTURE

One day Dink, went to his blue shed. He got in his suicide rocket. 'All systems, check, ice cream, check. Ten seconds to lift off … We're on Mars, yeah, let's party! Oh no - they're dynamite!' *Bang!* Was Dink still alive?
Ten years, twenty years on, nobody knows. What's that constellation?

Oliver Stacey (11)
Bampton CE Primary School, Bampton

LITTLE TIM

A long time ago, Fred Candy was an old snowman. He lived inside an igloo. He was thinking of going into a castle. In he went to look around. *Creak,* 'Boo!' A ghost stood right there.
Fred ran, 'Argh!' He tripped.
'Hello, it's me, Little Tim. I'm the ghost!'

Aaron Say (10)
Bampton CE Primary School, Bampton

THE CLIMB

This was the day that Jim and Bob were going to climb a mountain. An hour later they were going up the mountain and they heard the roar of the polar bear. After that they saw penguins. Then they found a cave which contained some secret treasure in a box!

Oliver Farmer (10)

Bampton CE Primary School, Bampton

THE CANE

It was empty, no teacher that day. That's what we thought. We all got left alone and then it happened. We were doing maths, I was stuck on a sum. So I asked Lucinda for help and our teacher came in and grabbed the cane and ... I woke up, shaking.

Alice Shuttleworth (10)

Bampton CE Primary School, Bampton

MOON WALK

I was being blasted into space fifty miles from the moon. What was that distant glow? We were getting closer. It was time for me to jump out with a parachute. *Whoosh!* Oh my gosh! The green alien was shooting cheese. It hit my head. 'Argh, Mum!' I woke up.

Jordan Strode-Grubb (11)

Bampton CE Primary School, Bampton

THE MUSEUM

It's night, the alarms are blaring. I rush to the museum but I see nothing wrong. The noise stops, I look, I'd better go. I hear a noise. I stop, I turn and I see the door opening. There's a light. I walk in. I see nothing. 'Surprise, happy retirement!'

Owen Tanner (10)

Bampton CE Primary School, Bampton

BUCKINGHAM NIGHTMARE

I was sprinting to Buckingham Palace in the mist. I leapt through the door and I raced down the shadowy corridor to get to my mum. I felt something tug at my leg, I tried to get away but I couldn't! I looked down quickly, it was a little corgi.

Molly-Jo Wright (10)

Bampton CE Primary School, Bampton

EYES OF THE WOODS

The woods were foggy and mysterious. George was feeling uncomfortable. He saw eyes looking at him. Something rustled in the bushes. The twigs snapped. He could hear voices behind and overhead. The moon was up by now, the wind slightly blew. The trees were waving, suddenly a rabbit appeared…

Dawid Sojka (11)

Bampton CE Primary School, Bampton

ONLY A NIGHTMARE

The mean, feisty spider is chasing after Alice. Run! Alice run! Quicker and quicker Alice runs. 'Help me!' The mean spider is getting hungry and it is going quicker. The spider has caught Alice! 'Argh!' Shouted Alice.
Thump! Thump! 'What happened?' gasped Mum! 'Don't worry it was only a dream.'

Oscar Smart (10)
Bampton CE Primary School, Bampton

LOST

I was lost on a planet, waiting to be picked up and taken home. Then suddenly there was a huge bang and a flash. I thought it was my ride home, then I heard jets. I looked, I saw my ship beaming me up from my mission. Commander Cody out.

Harry Trinder (10)
Bampton CE Primary School, Bampton

ONE STORMY NIGHT

There was an explorer who was climbing Mount Everest. The wind was high, the snow was heavy. Tons of snow came crashing down. The wind was getting heavier. He was getting higher and higher. He reached the summit but the wind was too strong for him and he fell. 'Argh!'

Thomas Pritchard-Pitts (11)

Bletchingdon Primary School, Bletchingdon

THIN ICE!

'Come on Lauren,' called Tom. 'Get your skates on.' 'No, I don't want to, the ice is too thin.' *Slip, bump, splash!* Tom struggled. He grabbed onto Lauren's leg. They tumbled into the freezing water, never to be seen again!

Alice Cormack (11)

Bletchingdon Primary School, Bletchingdon

THE WALK

As he walked up the mountain, all the other group members were miles away. 'Harry wait!' shouted Jane. Harry was at the summit. He waited there but there was no sign of the group. There was a strong wind. Harry shouted and screamed for help as he fell off the mountain.

Megan Pritchard-Pitts (10)

Bletchingdon Primary School, Bletchingdon

UNREAL NIGHTMARE?

One dark night on Planet Earth, a little boy was having a frightening nightmare. He was in a world where everything was made of stinky cheese. He couldn't take the horrible stench and woke up. Everything was made of stinky cheese.

Jacob Pickering (11)

Bletchingdon Primary School, Bletchingdon

THE DS GAME

One day, Bob was on his DS. Suddenly, he felt suction coming from his DS. He tried to hold it back but the suction was too powerful. He shut his eyes, then he opened his eyes. 'Where am I?' He looked around and realised he was in the game.

Joshua Harding (10)

Bletchingdon Primary School, Bletchingdon

SUPER TOAST MAN

One day, Jack wanted a piece of toast. It finished cooking, when a toast man popped out of the toaster and flew off to save the world. He flew past Hollywood, then Los Angeles, and hit Las Vegas. He saw the stratosphere and flew to the top. *Oh no.*

Harry Rolfe (9)

Bletchingdon Primary School, Bletchingdon

MERLIN

One horrible night, Merlin sat in bed, when Morgana knocked on the door then opened it. 'Merlin,' whispered Morgana.
'What?' said Merlin. It was so weird because she had a cat with her.
'Have a purrfect Halloween,' said the cat!

Lucy Carey (9)
Bletchingdon Primary School, Bletchingdon

THE NEW BABY

'They said they'd be here by 6:00 and its 6:30!' cried Sophie to her granny.
'They'll be here dear, just you wait,' replied Granny.
Five minutes later and headlights turned into the drive.
'They're here, they're here!' screamed Sophie, running to the back door. Mum had had a baby girl!

Lauren McLean (10)
Buckland CE Primary School, Buckland

FRIENDSHIP LAUGHTERS

One breezy day, Lucy came to the park to meet her friend called Rosie. When Lucy turned up, Rosie wasn't there. Lucy was confused. Lucy saw the bin rattle. *What's happening to the bin? Where's Rosie?* Lucy thought. Lucy walked closer. Someone came out, slowly, and it was Rosie.

Beatrice Economou (9)

Buckland CE Primary School, Buckland

UNTITLED

Echoing sounds whistle throughout the field as people cheer and laugh. Colours burst into bright sparks as the dying fireworks have their last chance to shine. Me and my dad are there alone because my mum died last 5th of November. That is why I remember the 5th of November.

Bethan Reynolds (9)

Buckland CE Primary School, Buckland

CAROL SINGERS

Knock, knock. I open the door. 'Who are you?'
'Don't you know? I said I was coming.'
'Well don't stand out there, come in.'
'It's not just me there's ... '
'How can there be more? I can only seat you.'
'We are not here for dinner. We are here to sing!'

Sam Gorham (10)
Buckland CE Primary School, Buckland

SHOCKING DREAM

'Where am I? What's going on?' I shout, but the words
mean nothing, for I have tape on my mouth and I am
strapped to an old, wooden chair with tough rope. A
dim light of a lamp is shining in my eyes. I wake, 'That
was a strange dream!'

Wilf Cartwright (10)
Buckland CE Primary School, Buckland

UNTITLED

Knock, knock. I rushed to the door, wondering who it could be on such a late night. Could it be Mum? 'No, because she's not back for half hour, and it can't be Dad because he's got a key.' Confused, Sam opened the door.
'Trick or treat?' said the boy.

Ben Loftus (10)

Buckland CE Primary School, Buckland

DYING MEMORIES

'She said she would be here, 6:00 on the dot. But no, there's no Mum!'
Finally the car comes, I hop in, about to yell and scream, but I don't. Suddenly I see a sodden face, a sad face. She peers at me and says, 'Sorry, Sasha's dead.' I cry!

Rebecca Le Maitre (10)

Buckland CE Primary School, Buckland

MERRY CHRISTMAS

Slowly, I opened my eyes, stunned to the spine, lying in my bed curled up, hoping there wasn't a murderer in the house. I looked at my alarm clock. The numbers said 6:32am. The door creaked open, my eyes were glued to it. 'Merry Christmas Megan,' shouted my parents happily.

Megan Meneer (10)

Buckland CE Primary School, Buckland

HEAVY HEARTED

I stumbled around in darkness, listening to the noises from outside. My heart pounded frantically. It felt so heavy, it was almost dragging me closer to the ground. By now, I was on my knees, desperately feeling for something to haul myself up. 'Zoey!' Dad suddenly burst in from nowhere.

Courtney Clements (11)

Buckland CE Primary School, Buckland

CHRISTMAS OR HALLOWEEN?

Bang ... The door shuddered downstairs. I'd been up in my bedroom wondering where my mum and dad were. *Ring* ... I couldn't answer this, why would I? I had to. I crept down the stairs, taking caution just in case someone was at the bottom. The door swung open, 'Merry Christmas!'

Amelia Jackson (10)

Buckland CE Primary School, Buckland

UNTITLED

Things started to crumble and slip through her fingers, leaving a hole in her heart like a wound that would never heal or like a knife being stabbed into her pounding chest. From that day onwards, she was depressed and distraught with various happenings of this sudden death.

Olivia James (10)

Buckland CE Primary School, Buckland

A NIGHTMARE!

Nervously, I just sat on my bed, alone. I saw the glinting lightning reach out to get me through my window. I heard drums of thunder roar and echo across the sky. I lay on my bed … afraid of the world. I woke up … It was just a mysterious dream!

Lydia McKenzie (10)

Buckland CE Primary School, Buckland

TRENCHES

Dear Diary,
I'm writing now as the bullets plunge into my fellows' hearts, crashing down in the freezing waters of the trench. There are Germans, cold, stiff, turning the trench water into a red. A minute ago the Germans tried to flank us, but we took them down fair and square.

Harry Robson (10)

Buckland CE Primary School, Buckland

IT'S YOU

Max got shoved down the dunes onto the beach, spitting out the sand. He looked up but the dark shapes were gone. He scurried up the beach. Max looked around, but no one. Suddenly Max heard footsteps, someone was behind him! He swung round, it was Gary. 'It's you!'

William Rainer (9)

Buckland CE Primary School, Buckland

NICE MONSTER!

'Bedtime!' Mum had shouted up to me. But I couldn't get to sleep. I was lying in my bed that night, thinking about a nice monster being my best friend. We told each other everything. Our secrets, our lives, even our crushes! But one day she left me all alone ...

Lauren Clements (9)

Buckland CE Primary School, Buckland

SHOPKEEPER'S GUARD DOG

Kaos was a big dog owned by a shopkeeper. He loved chasing people. One day after he chased a boy hanging around the shop Kaos' owner tied him up.

The next day the boy came back, Kaos barked and the owner ignored him. The boy ran away with expensive toys!

Joshua Bastille (9)

Burpham Primary School, Burpham

THE DRAGON'S ADVENTURE

One day Dave the dragon flew into a black hole which took him to Camelot. He found a boy called Merlin. Dave told Merlin he was a wizard, he'd teach him magic. Merlin was scared. Dave said, 'Don't be afraid, I won't eat you.' But he did eat him!

Henry Alden (9)

Burpham Primary School, Burpham

THE ATTIC

Emily was bored so she went up to the attic. When she got there she realised it was too dark so she decided to go down again. The door was jammed! She started shouting. When her mum got there it turned out the door was open the whole time.

Erin Caton (10)

Burpham Primary School, Burpham

WHERE IS EVERYONE?

The classroom was lonely. Kate thought everyone was there, but not a soul was there. She turned around and made her way to the door. Suddenly there was a weird sound. Kate was scared and uneasy. She then heard it again. Her friends were hiding from her.

Rithiga Rahulotchanan (9)

Burpham Primary School, Burpham

GHOSTS AND GHOULS

The house was empty, Jake was shivering with fear. Jake and Jack wanted to enter the old, abandoned house. It had been years since anyone had been in there. The only thing that stopped them was that it was said that it's haunted. 'Ghosts and ghouls fly out at night.'

Jake Vaughan (10)

Burpham Primary School, Burpham

THE HAUNTED HOUSE

There was once a haunted house where a knight came to life. A girl called Susan got chased by the knight. She soon realised that the knight just wanted to make friends with her. So soon the knight was friends with Susan forever. Soon it was dinner at Susan's house.

Rouma Cox (9)

Burpham Primary School, Burpham

THE BIRTHDAY ALONE

It was Katie's birthday but when she got home no one was there. *That's funny*, she thought. Then a door opened while she was crying. It was her mum. She asked her if she'd come into the kitchen. So a few minutes later she went in. 'Surprise!' What a birthday!

Cheryl Browne (9)

Burpham Primary School, Burpham

AN EXCITING ADVENTURE

I was trying to sleep but the excitement was too much. Suddenly I heard a whistle coming from outside. A large black train was puffing away. I ran downstairs and out the door. I climbed aboard the train. It was going to the North Pole to see Santa Claus.

Max Jones (9)

Burpham Primary School, Burpham

A CHRISTMAS SURPRISE

I lay in bed on Christmas Eve while I thought about all the presents. When I woke up there was nobody around. Then right in front of me I could see Santa Claus. He gave me a ton of presents and then he shouted, 'Merry Christmas to all and goodnight.'

Georgia Hughes (9)

Burpham Primary School, Burpham

THE LOST TRAIL

Peter woke with a fright. He heard a *whoosh!* He looked out the window and saw paw prints in the sand. He ran outside, breathing in the cold, misty air. Something wasn't right. Peter followed the tracks until they disappeared into the sea. Now Peter would never know what woke him.

Ben Spinks (9)

Burpham Primary School, Burpham

THE LITTLE ROBOT

All the other toys tease me. Just because I'm a robot and I speak differently. But today the toys were teasing me just like normal. Then suddenly one of the kids jumped in and put a new toy in the cupboard. I looked, and found that it was a robot!

Lauren Pellatt (9)

Burpham Primary School, Burpham

THE SPOOKY HOUSE

I was warned to never go there; the creepy mansion on the hill. On Halloween night, I tiptoed up the long driveway, imagining what horrors would be in there. I slowly pushed the door open and found myself facing an ugly witch. 'Trick or treat?' I shouted, hugging my auntie.

Holly Bond (9)

Burpham Primary School, Burpham

MARS 2035

It's 2035. The first man has walked on the Red Planet.
His family, the Franks, is very excited. Back on Mars
the astronaut feels a hot breath on the back of his neck!
He turns to see a red alien staring at him!
Then the alarm rings, it's a dream.

Luke Drummond (10)

Burpham Primary School, Burpham

ME AND MY DOG

Suddenly, I spun round, I thought I heard something,
but it was probably a hedgehog. I still had that feeling
that someone or something was watching me. I carried
on walking. Later on, when I was walking back from the
disco, something leapt out at me! It was my dog.

Liam Pearson (9)

Burpham Primary School, Burpham

THE STRAY DOG: A DAY IN THE LIFE OF ELLA

I was walking to school and saw a stray dog. My mum said she would take it to the local dog's home. I was thinking about the dog all day. When school finished I asked my mum if we could go back and get it but the dog was gone.

Ella Hinkley (9)

Burpham Primary School, Burpham

MAX'S MUM AND DAD

One day, a boy called Max, was walking alone when two icy and bony hands touched him. He froze. He ran, but the hands still touched him. When Max turned around, there in front of him were his mum and dad. They all went back to Max's house and partied.

Zoe Tickle (9)

Burpham Primary School, Burpham

BIRTHDAY SURPRISE

I woke up at six o'clock in the morning. I got out of my bed. I walked down the stairs. I heard a slight creak. I walked in the front room. There it was - I heard it again. I was frightened out of my life. 'Surprise! It's your birthday.'

Billy Fletcher (10)

Castle Primary School, Keynsham

HAUNTED

The ginormous house was dark and creepy. I walked up to it. 'Nooo!' said a friendly voice. I remembered Scott was behind me. 'You know everyone says this house is haunted.' I ran in, something was chasing me. Doors were slamming, something jumped out. 'Trick or treat?' It was Stella!

Emily Mayo (10)

Castle Primary School, Keynsham

SURPRISE

When I got home the door creaked. I was shivering. I heard some laughing. I screamed and the door opened. The lights flicked on and off. Loads of balloons came out of a box and 'Surprise!' It was my birthday. I'd just found out.
'Thank you for this great party!'

Jack Lillington (10)

Castle Primary School, Keynsham

BANG

There was something moving in the darkness. I couldn't see it because it was so dark at night. I wish I'd never heard it. It was terrifying, there was a gunshot then a scream. Then my brother jumped out with his popgun and shouted, 'Hands up!' What a relief.

Isabel Plucknett (10)

Castle Primary School, Keynsham

THE ADVENTURES OF DUCKY WUCKY!

Ducky Wucky isn't an ordinary duck, he's a hero. One day, he woke up and heard a lady screaming next door. It got closer and closer to him. It was his enemy, Catty Patty, holding a lady at knife point. Ducky saved her by fighting him off with bravery.

Preston Turner (10)

Castle Primary School, Keynsham

THE PLANE

It felt like my brain was going to explode. It was like I was pressurised. I pushed both my hands against my head. I closed my eyes really hard. I felt like I was going to explode. Then the boiled sweets came round. What a relief! Phew, I got worried.

Oliver Bates (10)

Castle Primary School, Keynsham

THE MYSTERY IN THE CAVE

Jack, Laura and Tom were on an adventure. They were friends who'd formed a gang called 'Let's Hunt!' Whilst exploring, they came across an old cave with a light shining at the far end. 'Let's hunt!' shouted Tom. Slowly entering, they were amazed to find a chest of golden treasure.

Chloe Doyle (10)

Castle Primary School, Keynsham

HELLRAISER

Leela was at the theme park with her friends, Charoz, Jess and Rio. They wanted to go on the ride, Hellraiser. She sat down on it and to her surprise a monster jumped out. She had to do something about it. Then she realised it was just a scary picture.

Charlotte Cherry (10)

Castle Primary School, Keynsham

DANGER BOARD

Ba-boom, ba-boom went Sally's heart, 'Come on Sally, you can do it!' went the crowd. As she got closer her legs were starting to feel like jelly. She felt as it she was going to fall to her death.
'It's just a diving board!' said Sally's swimming teacher.

Lauren Hopkins (10)

Castle Primary School, Keynsham

PUPPY LOVE

It was Thanksgiving, Sarah's favourite holiday. On Thanksgiving, she went to her local park. Every year she would meet her friend there - Tim, but he wasn't there. Suddenly there was a rustle in the branches. 'Surprise!' Tim jumped out and passed her the best present ever - a puppy!

Jessica Taylor (10)

Castle Primary School, Keynsham

ICE PHOENIX

The ice phoenix suddenly grabbed Lily by the hand and chucked her on the floor. Lily was scared, petrified. She couldn't believe what had happened. She stood up defiantly. She was going to beat the ice phoenix on her own, with only her pride. Her battle was about to begin.

Maili Nugent (10)

Chilton Primary School, Chilton

IT STRUCK AGAIN

It struck again. This time, she fainted onto the hard wooden floor. Blood was dripping off her forehead onto the floor, forming a red puddle. The poison was pushing all her blood out of her body. Maybe she survived the cruel experience, but maybe she didn't!

Caitlin Lee (10)

Chilton Primary School, Chilton

THE BOULDER

Indiana edged closer to the glistening gem on the high narrow ledge. Suddenly a rumbling, tumbling boulder came crashing through the highlands. Indiana tried to hurry himself but he couldn't. The rock knocked him off the mountain and into the forest below. How was he? Where was he?

Hannah Kellington (9)

Chilton Primary School, Chilton

THE BEAST

Spider the penguin was walking through the icy North Pole looking around for polar bears. Suddenly he heard a crack on the ice behind him. Spider spun around. It was a polar bear. He started running and he knew nowhere was safe for him to hide on the slippery ice.

Stephen Parry (10)

Chilton Primary School, Chilton

THE HAUNTED HOUSE

Ellie slowly grabbed the door with her shaking hand.
She opened the door slowly and there, standing right
in front of her, was the ghost. The ghost threw her onto
the floor. She could see blood, her blood. How was she
going to escape?

Holly Mulford (9)

Chilton Primary School, Chilton

THE GHOST

She woke. She felt someone grab her. It was a ghost. It
carried her to a distant land. Suddenly she was turning
see-through. She could only be a ghost. She haunted
her parents for years, until one day she visited no more.
Where could she have gone?

Ella Vincent (9)

Chilton Primary School, Chilton

THE BIRD

1924 October 27th
There are so many things different about me like, well I'm just like Sherlock Holmes. Most of the things I do are just solving problems, like once I discovered this kinda bird thing, I named it Griffin and for evermore I will be *dead* from the kill.

Callum Brailsford-Cox

Compass Point: South Street School, Bedminster

LOST IN A DESERT

The trickled grains of sand flew in my colossal eyes as I crunched the sand below my bare feet. In the distance; a hill, a flowing, dripping paradise giving astonishing illusion, full of magic. But until I was home my heart thumped with fear as I stood alone glumly.

Chazney Stokes (11)

Compass Point: South Street School, Bedminster

THE SCARY PHONE CALL

I dialled the number. No one answered. I dialled again.
No one answered. I was getting angry. Suddenly a girl
said, 'Hello.'
I said, 'Who is this?'
The girl said, 'My name's Mary, I'm a ghost girl.'
I got so scared I ran in my room and screamed,
'Argh.'

Perran Herbert (10)

Compass Point: South Street School, Bedminster

UNTITLED

'That thing is driving me crazy!' James said, 'It will look
like a hockey player when it comes out!'
At the end of the day Grandad told me it was going to
come out. So I put my hand in my mouth and I pulled
it out. 'Ow! that hurt.'

Isabella Stinson

Greatworth Primary School, Banbury

THE MISSING CAT

The front door had been left open. Where was the new kitten? I was really worried. He was not supposed to be outside yet. The search began. I searched upstairs, downstairs, outside, just in case. Then everywhere again, including all his favourite places. Finally there he was, under my bed.

Eleanor Faulkner (10)

Greatworth Primary School, Banbury

THE MYSTERY SHADOW

'Coming to find you!' shouted Tom. The floorboards creaked as he walked along them. The picture fell off the wall. Someone was there, but who? A shadow came from behind the door, but whose shadow was it? He crept towards the moving figure, closer and closer. 'Boo! Found you Lilly!'

Harriet Gibbs (10)

Greatworth Primary School, Banbury

THE TUNNEL RESCUE

Harvey ventured into the tunnel and came back terrified as he heard strange noises.

The following day he returned with his dad and a torch. Approaching for the second time, Harvey heard whimpering and they eventually discovered a fox trapped behind wire. They called the RSPCA who released it safely.

Harvey Woolmer (10)

Greatworth Primary School, Banbury

THE MYSTERY BOX

That night I ran home with excitement. I went straight to the living room. I was about to open the biggest present I had ever seen in my life! My hand reached up to the top of the box to rip off the paper but the label read … Mr. James.

Consuela James (10)

Greatworth Primary School, Banbury

DINOSAUR SURPRISE!

Jake woke with an uneasy feeling. Opening his eyes, he noticed a giganotosaurus chasing a triceratops around his bedroom. 'Help,' muttered Jake quietly, so the dinosaurs wouldn't notice him. 'Am I dreaming?' Cautiously, he opened his eyes wider and realised he was looking at his wall frieze. What a relief!

Jonty Joy (9)

Greatworth Primary School, Banbury

THE DRAGON'S SECRET

There was a scary, dangerous dragon who lived in a cave, he had a secret! A mouse moved in next door to the dragon. The mouse needed to borrow some sugar; he entered the dragon's cave. The dragon hid in the corner! Do you know what the dragon's secret is?

Geroge Coe (9)

Greatworth Primary School, Banbury

THE DRAGON

A dragon befriended William. Its teeth were long and yellow. Everywhere that William went the dragon was sure to follow. It stomped to the dentist with William one day, but that was against the dentist's rules, as dragons scare their patients away until there's no one left waiting at all!

William Peckover (10)

Greatworth Primary School, Banbury

TAKING THE PILLBOX

'Open fire!' said the General. 'Move out.' They were now at the edge of a pillbox. 'Attack, move in.'
'Fire, fire!' They'd shot everyone in the pillbox dead. The bomb was now planted. 'Run!' *Boom!* 'That was an easy job. Well done. Wait here for the reinforcements,' he commanded sternly.

James Deakin (11)

Greatworth Primary School, Banbury

A FISH TALE

I got my fish for Christmas. He was beautifully bright orange coloured; I loved him! One day, he was floating peculiarly in my fish tank. I was enormously worried! Mum knowingly whispered, 'When you wake up, he'll be fine.' Suddenly, like magic he sprung to life. He was just asleep.

Kieran Brady (11)

Greatworth Primary School, Banbury

THE GINGERBREAD MAN

One day Mrs. Baker made a gingerbread man. When he was cooked, she opened the cooker door and he jumped out, shouting, 'Run, run, as fast as you can, you can't catch me I'm the gingerbread man!' But he was wrong; she caught him and dunked him in her coffee.

Jazmyn Setty (9)

Greatworth Primary School, Banbury

THE SUN GOD'S SWORD

One day, I drank magic potion which made me as small as a mouse. I clambered on the back of a buzzard and soared across the frozen land into the sunset. The Sun God gave me a blazing sword of fire and I darted back through the starry sky.

Euan Edwards (8)

Greatworth Primary School, Banbury

MY LOTTERY PONY

I was so excited when I got my new pony called Diego. Mum had won the lottery and bought him for me. She had always promised me a pony if she won. I went into the stable to feed him but I woke up. It was all just a dream.

Sophie Barnett (8)

Greatworth Primary School, Banbury

SURPRISE!

Jim had arrived at karate lessons. He went inside to find a dark room. How very odd. Jim began to worry, had he got the wrong time? No, he couldn't have, it was definitely six. Jim started to shudder. Suddenly a whisper was heard ... 'Happy birthday!' What a great surprise!

Isabella Metcalfe (7)

Greatworth Primary School, Banbury

FATHER CHRISTMAS' ACCIDENT

On Christmas Eve, I put out some mince pies and carrots and put my stocking up. At midnight, Father Christmas suddenly fell to the ground when his sleigh broke. Luckily, he had a sack full of rope and tied the sacks to the reindeer who helped him deliver the presents.

Libby Deakin (8)

Greatworth Primary School, Banbury

GRIFFITHS

I was walking through a forest when a griffin landed. Although the griffin beautiful it is also dangerous I was so engrossed in looking at it that I didn't notice it ran towards me. It was friendly so I was able to fly it home. It became my pet.

Jessica Haggerty (8)

Greatworth Primary School, Banbury

GREAT YARMOUTH

It was a long drive to the seaside with Mum, Dad and Grandma. 'Are we there yet?' I said.
Mum said, 'I need the toilet.'
When we got there we went to the sealife centre. So many different things to see. It was getting late, time to head home.

Jessica Fee Maddox (7)

Greatworth Primary School, Banbury

THE DRAGON SLAYER

A knight in shining armour faces his dreaded enemy - a fierce dragon. He fights bravely and stabs the dragon in the heart. The dragon breathes its last fiery breath and the knight sets the princess free. They return to the castle on horseback, where they live happily every after.

Josh Hook (8)

Greatworth Primary School, Banbury

UNTITLED

The end of the dinosaurs was a long time ago. They lived on Earth for millions of years. They all died out when a comet hit the Earth. So I was surprised to see one in my back garden! It was huge. Then I realised it was a scary dream.

Katie Haggerty (7)

Greatworth Primary School, Banbury

MY BIRTHDAY

That sunny morning, I came downstairs and, without my parents knowing, I went into the living room to count how many presents. I heard a very, very strange noise, so I hid and spied on whoever it was. It was my mummy, so I ran upstairs!

Jack Youel (7)

Greatworth Primary School, Banbury

THE SCARE

Freddie was very fierce. He was never scared. It was a regular boring school day, but when I got to school he was horrified. It was so black in the terrifying school so he walked steadily to his classroom and a huge, horrific fright. No one was there, then ... 'Boo!'

Luci Griffith (9)

Greatworth Primary School, Banbury

SKY HEROES

I went to see my boss. I was told I had to do my training. I needed a plane and clothing before I did my mission - find a key to unlock the secret treasure chest. I found the chest and was about to open it, but Mum woke me up!

Luke Simpson (8)

Greatworth Primary School, Banbury

SUPER PIG!

Bang! 'What was that?' yelled Mr. Bacon. Then, with a flash of light he transformed into *Super Pig*.
'Ha, ha,' echoed around him.
'Oh no,' he exclaimed. 'That's The Mistress - she wants to destroy the world!' Then he ate some pork, his eyes turned green and he destroyed The Mistress!

Charlie Jay (7)

Greatworth Primary School, Banbury

THE RUGBY

On a Saturday we went to the Saints rugby match at Northampton. First the Saints scored a try then Leicester Tigers also scored a try. The Saints got possession of the ball on the restart and ran it two metres to score the winning try. We all went home happy!

Thomas Sinclair (9)

Greatworth Primary School, Banbury

CHRISTMAS CARDS

'Huh, I won't get those Christmas cards done before Christmas. It would be nice if Santa just came down the chimney and helped me ... Argh! Who's there?'
'Ho, ho, ho,' came the reply. We finished my cards and got them done before Christmas!

Benjamin Farmer-Webb (8)

Greatworth Primary School, Banbury

THE CURSE OF THE RED-EYED DOLL

It was car boot day and Amy was selling her little red-eyed doll because it gave her nightmares. When the car boot started, they couldn't find the doll. Suddenly, they heard screams and saw Dad being chased down the field by the doll. She lazered him and he died.

Megan Hart (8)

Greatworth Primary School, Banbury

THE KEY

A boy came home from school and he tried to get in but he couldn't. So he looked under the pot plants. It wasn't there! So he looked under the mat. It was there! So he opened the door. 'Yay!' he screamed.

Jack Brooks (8)

Greatworth Primary School, Banbury

UNTITLED

At the weekend I like to wake up early and go downstairs to use the PlayStation before breakfast. I like playing chess with Daddy. I like helping Mummy make cakes and licking the mixture out of the bowl. My favourite day ends when I have pizza for tea.

Rhys Ashford (7)

Greatworth Primary School, Banbury

SILLY SHOCK

Fairy Glen was an ordinary fairy. Suddenly he heard a noise. 'Argh! What's that noise?' Eventually he found out that it was only a bird. Now that was unacceptable. Was it really only a bird? Or a pigeon? Really that was weird.

Ben Prior (9)

Katesgrove Primary School, Reading

THE CONFUSION

One day, a boy called Kevin, was visiting the White House but his dad had found out that President Obama had been kidnapped. As they arrived at the huge gates, a security guard broke the news to Kevin. A huge limo parked up, out came Obama. It was confusion!

Eden Downes (10)

Katesgrove Primary School, Reading

THE DARK LONELY HOUSE

It was a dark, spooky night. A little girl named Annabelle, left all alone at home, scary shadows everywhere.
'Argh a zombie, argh, a ghost, argh!'
'Annabelle, what's all the fuss?' 'Argh, a zombie!'
'That's a tree.'
'Argh a ghost!'
'That's your cape on a hanger. Go to bed.'

Derice Charles (9)

Katesgrove Primary School, Reading

THE BANGING DOOR...

It was dark, Halloween night. Emma was home alone. There was a loud bang on the door. *Bang, bang, bang!* Emma peered through the small window and saw gruesome goblins and bleeding children. Emma screamed with fright. The door bashed open. 'Trick or treat?'

Shisam Gurung (9)

Katesgrove Primary School, Reading

PERMISSION

One day Zak walked in a forest. While he was walking he thought someone was following him. He was scared out of his socks. As he turned round, shaking, his mum jumped out of nowhere and said, 'Where do you think you're going without permission? You're grounded for a year!'

Zaki Gulzar (9)

Katesgrove Primary School, Reading

THE BEST BIRTHDAY EVER

One dark Halloween night, Lucy went walking, suddenly someone tapped her. She turned around and saw it was her friend. 'Oh you scared me,' said Lucy. They saw a dark house close by and went in.
They went upstairs and when Lucy opened the door, everyone shouted, 'Happy birthday Lucy!'

Asmita Gurung (9)
Katesgrove Primary School, Reading

SPACE CADETS

'Mum, we're going to the park,' said Eddie and Lee. They went to a rocket ship instead. Just then Lee slipped and fell on the launch button.
Cautiously stepping out, both were on a planet. Eddie and Lee looked down and 'Surprise.' They were just in a new space museum.

Umayr Raja (9)
Katesgrove Primary School, Reading

SURPRISE!

One evening, Claire went to the bungalow that her uncle owned. It was haunted. Creeping sounds were getting nearer. She went inside. Claire was scared because no one was there. The creaking noise came again. She switched the lights on and ... 'Happy birthday!' It was only her family.

Shilpi Sanyal (10)

Katesgrove Primary School, Reading

TRAPPED!

It was a hot day in Egypt. A little girl called Lucy went to see the famous pyramids. She took an icy bottle of water. Finally she reached the biggest pyramid. Suddenly the pyramid door started to shut. She was trapped! Luckily her house key opened the secret door.

Amima Ahmed (9)

Katesgrove Primary School, Reading

SHADOWS

Alex enjoyed cycling. He noticed shadows marching towards him. Then a petrifying humming sound rang in his ears. He tried to outrun them but there were too many. The shadows were revealed and ... It was only his friends playing a trick on him with their remote controlled zombies.

Baraka S. K. Kajatto (9)

Katesgrove Primary School, Reading

SURPRISE FROM MUM AND DAD CREEPY

My house was dark when I appeared from school. 'Hendry, Hendry ...' I heard someone calling. I went in. It was very spooky. I shouted, 'Mum? Dad? Where have you gone? Come back please.' I heard something. They suddenly put on the light. 'Surprise!'
'Wow! What a great surprise birthday party.'

Kevin Emmunal Francis (11)

Katesgrove Primary School, Reading

GABRIELLA AND THE KEY

Flickering figures haunted Gabriella, as she stepped into the vile woods. In the distance was a glow, a key. She grabbed it, a dragon appeared. He licked his thin, crusty lips. She snatched the cut-throat dagger from her pocket and slit his head. She never forgot that day.

Ivan Neil De Guzman (10)

Katesgrove Primary School, Reading

CINEWORLD

Charz wanted to go to a movie because she hadn't been for ages! So she decided to go by herself. When she arrived, at Cineworld, she looked at the time from nine, straight to twelve! The lights went out! A scream was heard. 'Aarrgghh!' Someone kidnapped her … !

Sanya Hussain (11)

Katesgrove Primary School, Reading

A LOVELY SURPRISE

He turned the key silently. As he crept into the house lowering his luggage, he heard a creak. What was behind him? Quickly, he turned around. Nothing! There were baubles covering the floor. 'Surprise! Merry Christmas!' everyone cheered.

Chirag Vijay (11)

Katesgrove Primary School, Reading

THE TERRIFYING BEDROOM

'Sarah, time for bed,' said Dad quietly. As soon as she got upstairs she found a key in front of her room. As she bent to get it she was grabbed and pulled into her room. Luckily her mum heard her and helped. In the end she moved her bedroom.

Stephanie George (10)

Katesgrove Primary School, Reading

THE GIRL WHO NEVER LISTENS

There once was a silly girl, her name was Shara. She would always go to the library. *Bash!* The till manager came running towards Shara. The manager saw books all over the floor. The manager said 'Not again!' she was a really lucky girl who got away with it easily.

Kiran Masood (10)

Katesgrove Primary School, Reading

UNTITLED

One shiny day, Lucy was in her cottage alone. Later on that day, Lucy heard the doorbell ring. She nervously walked ahead. It was a ghost! She screamed so loud. Luckily, she kicked him out the door and he never came back. Eventually Mum and Dad came home.

Hashim Shafiq (10)

Katesgrove Primary School, Reading

TINY THOMPSON

Big elephants can't always use small exits because they are so large, so when Thompson went through a door he was very shocked because this door was very small. He saw a balloon: 'Happy Birthday Thompson,' and a big hatch with his name on for him to go through later.

Beatrix Shephard (9)

Kingham Primary School, Chipping Norton

SANTA

On Christmas Eve, Santa came down the chimney but no one was there. He heard a creak from the wooden floor. He heard another noise coming from the kitchen. As he got there, he had a surprise. It was the people. They all had a party and went to bed.

Joshua Skea (8)

Kingham Primary School, Chipping Norton

THE PONY

He looked at my pockets, hoping there was a treat lurking in there. I rattled his head collar and somehow managed to put it on. I led him out, saddled him, then forced the bit into his mouth and mounted. We cantered down the field and then we were free.

Beth Wilkinson (9)

Kingham Primary School, Chipping Norton

THE SEAS

In the sea, sharks stalked. Fish swum calmly. Ships sailed on the water. Then, where the sharks and fish were was turned into a bloodbath. The fish attacked the sharks! The people on the ship were scared, then there was a whole load of fish jumping out of the sea.

Euan Fisher (7)

Kingham Primary School, Chipping Norton

A WALK IN THE WOODS

I walked through the woods one night, with a full moon shinning through the clouds. I heard footsteps come closer and closer, a shiver came down my spine. Something, or someone, was touching my back. I turned around and screamed, but there was nothing, so I ran into the night.

Izzy Nash (11)

Kirtlington Primary School, Kirtlington

JEOPARDY!

Down the slimy tunnel crept Joe, slipping on the moss and primordial ooze dripping from the weathered walls. There was a glow of fiery orange in the distance and he suddenly felt hot. Just then, a deafening roar smashed the silence. He was slipping, down towards the mouth of Vyperax ...

Craig Fasanmade (11)

Kirtlington Primary School, Kirtlington

A DAY IN THE LIFE OF JIM

Jim was walking down the street. The smell hit him straight away. It danced up his nose. He followed the smell. It took him round corners, across roads, until finally, he stood outside the bakers. He walked in and said, 'Please can I have that blue door?'

Alex Vickars (10)

Kirtlington Primary School, Kirtlington

WAR ZONE?

Sam faced the terrible noise. In front of him hundreds of soldiers fought a war. He was very scared of the machine guns pinning bullets into the men's hearts. 'Well?' said a mysterious voice.
'Sorry Dad, can you turn the telly down? I'm trying to do my homework,' said Sam.

Harrison Woodin-Lygo (10)

Kirtlington Primary School, Kirtlington

THE BOY WHO WAS SHOCKED

One day, Tim came home. It was silent. He looked up at the top of the staircase. It was dark and silent. He went upstairs and opened the first door but nothing was there. So Tim went to the next room, nothing there. But - 'Happy Birthday Tim!' Tim was shocked.

Connie Morley (11)

Kirtlington Primary School, Kirtlington

THE HORRIBLE HAUNTED HOUSE

There was a haunted house and if entered, you never came out. A girl went in but never came out and everyone had been looking for her. The Police went in there, they did come out. They said, 'It's nothing. They're just camping and having a jolly laugh!'

Charlotte Pinker (9)

Kirtlington Primary School, Kirtlington

THE BOY

Tom walked to the shops to buy some sweets and he could buy sweets or chocolate. So he went back home and looked in the fridge to see if he had chocolate or sweets and he had chocolate. So he ran to the shop and brought sweets.

Erin Day (9)

Kirtlington Primary School, Kirtlington

MICE RUNNING, CATS LEAPING

Mouse running as fast as it can. The cat leaping around in the air trying to get the mouse. It runs past the dog's home, the cat runs past the dog's home but the dog comes running out! It just misses and the mouse just escapes and lives forever.

Libby Pritchard (9)

Kirtlington Primary School, Kirtlington

ALIEN IN THE WOODS

John was walking in the forest. A green glow lurked alone in the trees. John parted the leaves. An alien foraged in the undergrowth. Scared for his life John ran. He heard the alien running after him. He climbed a tree. When morning came, the alien was waiting and ate him.

Myles Greatbatch (9)

Kirtlington Primary School, Kirtlington

SANTA WATCH

John stood outside looking into the sky. He had tried to tell his Mom Santa wasn't real. She didn't believe him. She told him to watch the sky. An aeroplane passed overhead. He heard footsteps behind him and felt a breath on his neck ... 'We wish you a Merry Christmas!'

Grace Henstone (10)

Kirtlington Primary School, Kirtlington

THE MIDNIGHT MURDERER

Chloe crept through Tremblewood forest. She was lost in the midnight hour and lurking about was the midnight murderer. There was a crunch, Chloe started to run when suddenly she bumped into someone. Oh no it could be the midnight murderer! Moonlight shone upon the shape. 'Mum,' Chloe cried.

Vicky Grimshaw (11)

Kirtlington Primary School, Kirtlington

SPACE WARS

'In here,' said the general. The spaceman dived away from the shooting. We went to the king's room through a tunnel, aliens saw us. We shot them but they had called for help. More aliens came and pinned us to the wall. *Game Over* went the video game.

Jacob Short (9)

Kirtlington Primary School, Kirtlington

CREEPY HOUSE

The girl was alone outside. She saw a house. She went inside, up the stairs. She saw a shadow. She stopped. She followed slowly.
She heard a noise. So she ran downstairs out the door. She felt something on her back. She turned round and it was just a twig!

Megan Bickley (10)
Kirtlington Primary School, Kirtlington

THE RUN

I was running through the woods when I heard a whistle, and then running feet. I heard a loud shout from behind me. It turned into a scream. I ran but it was catching up. I stopped. It was my angry PE teacher telling me to get back on the field.

Cerys Cherry (10)
Kirtlington Primary School, Kirtlington

EXAM NERVES

I ran, the wind pushing with a force I did not know it had, the trees scratching at my face. I had to rest, so I stopped and turned and wished I had not, for there in the shadows was my teacher with a maths SATs paper, rubber and pencil!

Zoë Brown (9)

Kirtlington Primary School, Kirtlington

PANICKING

I was running, panicking, out of breath. I searched everywhere, every speckle, every spot, in and out of the classrooms, past the teachers, past the pupils. I was running out of time. I had to move faster, but I couldn't. Then I found the water fountain. I was saved!

Lauren Moss (10)

Kirtlington Primary School, Kirtlington

MY EVIL MUM

I was sprinting as fast as my legs could carry me, the branches trying to hold me back. I struggled through quickly. I stopped to catch my breath but there was no time. I turned round to see my evil Mum with the horrible greens and the dust pan. 'Argh!'

Poppy Macfarlane (9)
Kirtlington Primary School, Kirtlington

TRAPPED

I was running and running. I couldn't stop. I kept going, not daring to look. Then I saw my Mum with my clock. 'Bedtime,' she said. I ran away and there was my Dad with my homework. I didn't know where to go. I was trapped.
I shouted, 'Help me!'

Georgia Lay (9)
Kirtlington Primary School, Kirtlington

JUNGLE

In a green, musical jungle, animals all around, a lion goes roar; a monkey sings, 'oo-aa-oo-aa.' I go on my adventure to find a volcano. I saw the volcano; it starts to erupt. There are so many bangs and splashes; bits of lava. It's a beautiful sight.

Niamh Baber (10)

Pensford Primary School, Pensford

I WISH

It was December, everyone was getting ready for the big day, except one little girl named Lilly; she was in the orphanage waiting to be adopted. 'Please, I would really love a family this Christmas Santa please.' Lilly wished, as she sat on her uncomfortable bed. Lilly's wish came true!

Poppy Moore (10)

Pensford Primary School, Pensford

GOBBLES' STORY

Once there was a turkey named Gobbles. He was a very hungry turkey. One day, he spotted some lovely looking fresh green sprouts, so he decided to go and pinch one or two. He was about a centimetre away from the closest sprout and all of a sudden, *Bang!*

Phoebe Wilcox (11)

Pensford Primary School, Pensford

THE SCARED GIRL

The girl creeped through the house and wondered why it was so quiet. It seemed like a haunted house; the girl was really scared. Then she heard the door squeak open. Who was that? Then she realized it was her parents planning a secret party for her.

Bebhinn Baber (10)

Pensford Primary School, Pensford

PARTY TIME

Ding dong at the door. 'Oh Mum, do you think it is what I have been hoping for? Because I am just bursting to see my friends!'
'Happy birthday.'
'Oh thank you everybody for coming. Come on everybody, let's party to death!'
'Yeah.'
'I love you.'

Olivia Howlett (8)
St John's RC Primary School, Banbury

TV ADVERT FAILURE

'Break a leg!' shouted the director. The man focused himself and walked into the view of the camera.
'I'm fluffy the dog and here to … oops!' he shouted as he fell over.
'Let's try again tomorrow and by the way I didn't mean literally break a leg,' explained the director.

Christopher Watson (8)
St John's RC Primary School, Banbury

UNTITLED

'You come here after school to the old terrifying house
OK?'
'Yes Mum,' said Jake …
'Hooray! School, Boo it's shut!'
Mum told me to meet her here, why is there a shadow
and why did I just hear a creak?
'Surprise.'
'Mum, you made me jump.'
'Happy birthday.'

Martin Ryder (8)

St John's RC Primary School, Banbury

SPOOKY SURPRISE

Lauren came into school. She thought, *where is
everyone, it is Monday?* The lights were off. She
couldn't turn them on. There were shadows that looked
like ghosts. She thought,, *no it must be a dream.* She
saw it was a ghost. She turned the lights on. 'Surprise!'
shouted everyone.

Arabella Cummings (8)

St John's RC Primary School, Banbury

SPOOKY SURPRISE

Caitlin woke up in a dark and spooky house all alone.
'I'm scared. I thought Mum and Dad would know it's
my birthday.' She walked down the creaky stairs.
Caitlin thought her mum and dad had disappeared or
been abducted by aliens. A door opened. She walked
through.
'Surprise!'
'Thanks.'

Alex Murphy (8)
St John's RC Primary School, Banbury

MONKEY BUSINESS

One day at the zoo a monkey escaped. The monkey
was causing mayhem inside the London shopping
centre. The monkey's name was Markie. The police
almost got him. Markie was too fast for them. One dived
on Markie. He got him and he took Markie back.

Tyrell Intsiful (8)
St John's RC Primary School, Banbury

THE STRANGE NOISE

'What's that strange noise? I'm going mad,' Jack whispered.
'No you're not,' said the weird mystery voice.
'Uh - Who's that?'
'Me, Grandad Charlie,' Dad said.
'I never had a grandad Charlie,' Jack said.
'Yes you do, your mum's dad. He was called Joe ... I tricked you!'

Daniel Murphy (8)

St John's RC Primary School, Banbury

CHOCOLATE DIVA!

Lydia loved chocolate, so she went to a candy shop and bought a bar of chocolate. After she had finished her bar of chocolate, everything she touched turned to chocolate. Soon everything in Frankfurt was chocolate. 'Mmm, yummy.' The chocolate started to melt. 'Oh no, my chocolatey land!'

Bryony Jien (8)

St John's RC Primary School, Banbury

THE GHOST!

The door was open a crack, Mum had disappeared. Liz was afraid. Liz didn't dare move a muscle in her body. She heard a noise. It was coming from the living room. She went inside. The noise got louder ... There was a ghost! 'Surprise!' It was Mum underneath a sheet!

Elysia Roadnight (8)

St John's RC Primary School, Banbury

THE WHITE CATASTROPHE

When Clive, the manager, got to the shop he was stunned. There'd been a snowstorm. The whole shop was white with snow ... at least it looked like snow.
'What's happened?' Clive said.
'Don't worry,' the employee said. 'It's only a foam machine malfunction.'
'How we ever gonna clean this?'

Luke Broughan (8)

St John's RC Primary School, Banbury

CHRISTMAS TROUBLE

It's Christmas Eve. I can't wait for tomorrow. I can't wait for presents, Christmas dinner, my stocking filled, staying with my family and the New Year. But look around, there are no decorations. Wait - I can hear a twinkling, let's be really quiet. The Christmas fairy has been. Hooray! Hooray!

Eliese Johnson (8)

St John's RC Primary School, Banbury

MY FAVOURITE PRESENT

Out of bed, run to the garden, have a little warm up. I'll jog around the garden for a few minutes. Go back in the garden, I've heard a knock on the door. Oh it's my mum and dad. That's a present for me!

Nicola Guarin (8)

St John's RC Primary School, Banbury

COOL CAITLIN'S PARTY

Cool Caitlin was at her birthday party. Anxious Alex was invited to cool Caitlin's party but he didn't have any trunks. So he went shopping. When he got to the shopping centre, jealous John had got Alex pink trunks! When Alex got there he was embarrassed.

Caitlin Marron (8)

St John's RC Primary School, Banbury

DING DONG

Ding dong. I opened the door. This tall, angry babysitter was at the door. 'I'm looking after you.'
'Nooooo!' I ran upstairs and slammed the door. *Can this be happening to me?* I thought.
Mum and Dad came back from their restaurant. 'We were just playing,' said the angry liar.

Mia Grossi (8)

St John's RC Primary School, Banbury

SANTA CLAUS

It was Christmas Eve in Oxford. Kenan and Kel were getting ready for Santa Claus. People were making Christmas cake. But Kenan and Kel would not go to sleep. Finally they went to sleep. It was midnight. Kenan and Kel saw Santa Claus and they shared the cake with him.

Madeline Lillis (8)

St John's RC Primary School, Banbury

LITTLE MISS MUFFET

Little Miss Muffet sat on a rock under a tree eating a bowl of porridge. A spider came and made Little Miss Muffet run away. But she left her bowl. The bowl broke. The spider said, 'It's time to eat. I like eating. It's just a pleasure to eat.'

Iéléna Héraud (8)

St John's RC Primary School, Banbury

BEACH ADVENTURES

Biff and Rose went to the beach because their mums said to. When they got there, it was full of people. The tide came in. Two children were in the water. Rose and Biff went in to help them. They took them to the hospital, then went home to play.

Natasha Gamu Tsatsa (7)

St John's RC Primary School, Banbury

THE ALIEN

The alien lived at a very scary house. It was really creepy. The alien thought there was a monster in his house because he heard whispering in a room. He opened the door and saw the monster. They had a fight and the alien won.

Alex Napierkowski (7)

St John's RC Primary School, Banbury

DANGER DUNGEONS

One day fearless Fred came across a building disguised as a castle. Fred, being fearless, went inside but he was walking into the most dangerous dungeon of all. He drank blood thinking it was Ribena, and then he saw ghosts. 'Wake up, school time,' Fred heard. He rushed downstairs.

Amelie Lamprecht (7)

St John's RC Primary School, Banbury

ELEPHANT

Rhino and Elephant went for a walk. Rhino found a box, he opened the box. Elephant went in the box; he ended up in a new world. He had an adventure. Then the world started to spin. He fell asleep and when he woke up he was at home.

Luca Lenihan-Orwa (7)

St John's RC Primary School, Banbury

THE ICE CREAM VAN

Once there was a van. Not any old van, an ice cream van. But one day, it ran away and then it was in England. It made the best ice creams in the world. Everyone kept on buying them until one day, they ran out!

Penny Higham (7)

St John's RC Primary School, Banbury

MONSTER UNDER THE BED

Thomas went to bed. A monster jumped out. Thomas was so terrified that he ran downstairs and hid under a dark chair. The monster followed him and found Thomas, and he would have eaten Thomas, only he was afraid of the dark place under the chair.

Thomas Fairley (7)

St John's RC Primary School, Banbury

PIXIE PATHS

Kelly was walking home, when she heard something in the bushes! Kelly was frightened. She thought it might be a monster but when she looked it was a pixie. Kelly ran home and when she arrived, 'Surprise.' It was a pixie party and all her friends were there.

Olivia Gritton (7)

St John's RC Primary School, Banbury

SPACE ADVENTURE

One day Dave and Alan went to the moon and met an astronaut. They spoke to the astronaut and he seemed like a nice guy. They had a little chat and went back to Earth. They told everyone but no one believed them.

Aidan Christie (8)

St John's RC Primary School, Banbury

A BIG DOCTOR SURPRISE

Polly had to go to the doctors. Polly was scared, she did not know what doctors were like. All morning she was scared and frightened. Her mom had to nearly drag her down the street. She cried in the waiting room, but surprise! Polly's uncle Ben was the doctor!

Lizzie Jenkins (7)

St John's RC Primary School, Banbury

TOILET

Once upon a time, a toilet came to life. When the people sat on it, the seat flipped up and they fell in. Then it flushed itself. The people got fed up with this, so they filled him with soil and planted flowers.

Angus Paviour (7)

St John's RC Primary School, Banbury

PRINCESS PROBLEMS

A princess went out. It was dark and gloomy. She heard a bell ring 12 times over. She ran home in fright. 'Mummy, Mummy!' she said. 'It's midnight, I'm going to turn into a pumpkin.'
'Oh darling,' her mum said.

Megan Veres (7)

St John's RC Primary School, Banbury

PIXIE LOTT

One day, Pixie Lott saw loads of paths and went down the wrong one. It led to the palace where the royal family lived. It was dark and spooky. The lights turned on, Pixie Lott ran. She saw a ghost. The ghost turned into a sugar mouse, Pixie Lott ate it.

Antonia Strachan (7)

St John's RC Primary School, Banbury

PIXIE PATHS

Once upon a time there lived some little pixies. Their home was under a waterfall. They splashed around happily all day long. They liked to explore. One day they went on a walk into a big magical cave. They found a button and pressed it. They appeared at the waterfall.

Evie Timbrell (7)

St John's RC Primary School, Banbury

TALENTED MONKEYS

Star was a monkey. The talent show came to town. Star wanted to go on the talent show but she had no talent. Amba put some ice down Star's back. Then Star started to dance. The talent show company came. They gave her the trophy and she won the award.

Matilda Thornton (7)

St John's RC Primary School, Banbury

UNTITLED

The unicorns live in a magical land under a waterfall. One day, a unicorn called Lucy disappeared. All of the unicorns looked. At last, her dad said, 'We've got half an hour or she will lose her magic.' Then suddenly her mum found her asleep in a cave. *Zzz.*

Evelyn Harwood (7)

St John's RC Primary School, Banbury

GHOST SURPRISE

Once there was a boy he had just got home and opened the door. Suddenly he saw ghosts coming out of the lounge, spiders hanging off the ceiling. Then his parents jumped down with his friends. 'Happy Halloween,' they said.

Edward Andrews (7)

St John's RC Primary School, Banbury

HAPPY HALLOWEEN!

I came out of my bedroom. I looked out of the window and I saw a black figure standing outside my house. I went downstairs and opened the door very slowly. I slammed the door. I was too scared. I took a breath, I opened the door. 'Happy Halloween!'

Archie Griffin (9)

St John's RC Primary School, Banbury

THE ASCENT AND DESCENT

The plane shot up. His heart racing. Two planes came from behind; Benecio hammered the controls back, a vertical ascent turned into a vertical descent. The planes behind had gone. 'Phew, we're safe,' Benecio said with a sigh of relief. But Simon Madison was still in existence …

Thomas Allman (10)

St John's RC Primary School, Banbury

DINOSAUR INVASION

While I was at home I was invaded by dinosaurs. Stegosaurus popped out from behind the armchair. Pterodactyl flew over my head, T-rex nearly trod on me. I ran out of the door and quickly shut myself in the shed, but there was Diplodocus. How would I ever get away?

Kyle Miller (10)

St John's RC Primary School, Banbury

TRICK OR TREAT

Lucy opened the gate, *sqeeakkk* ... went the gate. Lucy walked through the green, dark garden. Owls whistling, birds squawking, red eyes glowing around the garden. Lucy's heart raced. She sprinted into the creepy house and there were blood, fangs, goblins etc. There came a loud thundering noise ... 'Trick or treat?'

Callum Timbrell (10)

St John's RC Primary School, Banbury

ALONE

I climbed up high, the highest I'd ever got before. I then remembered watching my dad from the bottom. When I leant on the pyramid, the pyramid slid open. I fell. I landed on the solid ground. I got up and wandered around. I was alone, trapped in the pyramid.

Sophie Mitchelmore (9)

St John's RC Primary School, Banbury

HE'S NOT KIDDING

'Argh' said Jake. Doesn't matter, he screams all the time, over nothing at all ... Actually he's not kidding. There's a bunch of tiny evil monkeys, scary, hairy beasts. Blood is everywhere they try to eat Jake but they only get as far as the tip of his little toe.

Lewis Langan (10)

St John's RC Primary School, Banbury

THE LAUGH

I heard it, a laugh. A sly, sneaky laugh coming from the attic, it sounded just like Tom, but no, it couldn't be. It must have just been my imagination. Aunty Cath called up, 'Izzy, Soph, it's time to go to bed.' I heard the laugh, but this time louder.

Molly Walsh (10)

St John's RC Primary School, Banbury

PLANE NIGHTMARE

I was finally going abroad. We checked in and got seated in the plane. The plane took off. We were above the ocean when one of the engines blew up. Both wings were hit off by two other planes passing by. We dived, it was the end of our lives.

Aodhan O'Sullivan (10)

St John's RC Primary School, Banbury

THE SCREAM

We were coming in from play time. We heard a scream, nobody was there. Time passed and it was so quiet, we could hear a pin drop. All of a sudden, we heard a scream. A whistle of the wind flew into the classroom door. 'Diana I'm coming, beware, beware.'

Katie-Anna McAnulty (10)

St John's RC Primary School, Banbury

ALL ALONE IN THE WORLD

Oliver sat up and gazed around the room. He remembered his mother; how she died; how he was sent to the workhouse, and how his life had been turned upside down. Suddenly he realised he was alone in the world. All hope of family; dead. All hope of friends; dead.

Mae French (10)

St John's RC Primary School, Banbury

THE SHIVER!

I sat up, I could not get to sleep. My spine shivered, 'I'm coming to get you!' It said again. The wind whistled. I lay down to get to sleep. But something kept on haunting me. Who was it? Was it really real? Or could it just be my imagination?

Holly Castle (10)

St John's RC Primary School, Banbury

GHOSTS!

'Did you hear something?' Aunt Gwen asked.
Uncle Peter stupidly replied, 'You're mad.' Funnily Uncle Peter heard something. 'Your madness is contagious, I thought I heard something.'
Quickly the children burst in and said simply, 'Ghosts!'
Suddenly a horrific, giant, cackle came, but they were all too scared to speak!

Emilia Lillis (10)

St John's RC Primary School, Banbury

SPOOKY ALICE

Alice was laughing; Uncle Peter heard her and nervously laughed. Aunt Gwen was not laughing at all because the last few days had been strange. The doors had been opening and closing by themselves! Aunt Gwen knew there was someone or something lurking in the house; was it evil?

Zoe Hastings (10)

St John's RC Primary School, Banbury

OLIVER TWIST

As Oliver tried to snuggle into the old, ripped blanket and boarded bed, he was looking at different kinds of bunks. He sat up and started to cry, but hid his tears. He lay back down and stopped crying, because Fagan was looking at him with a very sad face.

Sadie Donaghy (10)

St John's RC Primary School, Banbury

OLIVER TWIST

As Oliver sat there, tucked up in a cosy basket with a thin scruffy sheet pulled over him, he thought about Dodger; all the friends he had made; Fagin's warm welcome. Everyone had been so kind to him. Oliver could not wait to start to explore London the next day.

Louisa Higham (10)

St John's RC Primary School, Banbury

STAR FLIGHT

'Captain's log, star date 13:95. We are approaching magma and are waiting for the blast, the blast of an ion cannon. It will burn our ship. We must stay alert!'
'Captain, we need you on the bridge,' said the co-pilot. *'Red alert, red alert!'* The captain ran. Death!

Connor Marron (10)

St John's RC Primary School, Banbury

THE VOICE

Lucy heard a voice. She steadily walked to the attic but nobody was there. The voice came back again.
'Who's there?'
'It's me, Alice.' She was wearing some old-fashioned clothes. Lucy ran down, Alice followed her the whole way. Lucy looked behind her; Alice had left and was nowhere.

Sophie Pearce (10)
St John's RC Primary School, Banbury

A CHRISTMAS DREAM

Megan went to bed on Christmas night and dreamed of a teddy bear. In her dream, she saw Santa. She'd always wanted to. She woke up the next day and found a teddy bear-shaped present under the tree. 'Merry Christmas.'

Bronwyn Miner (9)
St John's RC Primary School, Banbury

HALLOWEEN SPECIAL!

Bob was at home on Halloween. The door banged three times. He opened the door and no one was there. Suddenly Bob was scared to death. There were blood-dripping wolves, vicious vampires. He got a reply of, 'Happy Halloween.' He gave out sweets and one bit him.

Jake Kelly (8)

St John's RC Primary School, Banbury

UNTITLED

I was walking outside all alone. Then a strange man in a hoody came up to me and then tied me to a truck. Suddenly, I woke up and told my dad I'd had a bad dream. 'But last night you didn't fall asleep …'

Neo Kalungu-Banda (8)

St John's RC Primary School, Banbury

SHREK SAVES DONKEY

One day Shrek was stomping through the forest and saw a donkey being chased by villagers. When they were really close he decided to beat them up. When he rescued Donkey he noticed how annoying he was so at 12 o'clock he kicked Donkey out of his house!

Jamie Monaco (8)

St John's RC Primary School, Banbury

THREE CITY PIGS

Once upon a time there were three pigs who built together, at Halloween, an iron and steel house. They were proud of it. They strolled out and came home and saw a bloody tooth and a furry dress like a wolf. But it was their mum saying, 'Beautiful house!'

John Carlo Dimaculangan (8)

St John's RC Primary School, Banbury

UNTITLED

After school I went home to my street which I live in. suddenly a dark mist came. Then a strange figure came out - it looked like a dragon! Then I rushed home. I looked at the time - it was twelve. I saw out the window the dragon was my dad!

Ezekiel De Luna (8)

St John's RC Primary School, Banbury

THE CAVEMAN TOOTH FAIRY WHO CAN NOT FLY AT ALL

One day, a caveman becomes a tooth fairy but he can not fly. He takes the teeth but he gives them no money, so all the kids are really sad. They are ashamed of the tooth fairy. The tooth fairy does not like being a tooth fairy at all!

Sophie Short (8)

St John's RC Primary School, Banbury

THE WORST HALLOWEEN EVER!

Once there was a girl who lived in a wood and there was a cottage. It was the least spookiest Halloween ever. The cottage was given a curse. It was turned into a mansion. There was a knock at the door, the door opened and ... It was a chicken!

Isabella Hill (8)

St John's RC Primary School, Banbury

THE NIGHT BEFORE CHRISTMAS

In a dark, scary and haunted house, lived a boy called Callum. Callum's mum and dad abandoned him after he made bad medicine. Callum heard something upstairs. It was coming closer. 'Argh!' Callum screamed. He fainted.

Kalim Saddiq (9)

St John's RC Primary School, Banbury

FERNEO THE MOUNTAIN FIRE DRAGON

Once there was a little boy called Timmy, he liked playing knights. One day there was a big storm all over the village. Everyone was afraid of it. The little boy saw a beast. He found some armour and then he started a fight. He was powerful.

William Hastings (8)

St John's RC Primary School, Banbury

THE ICE CREAM SHOP

A crazy man was at the ice cream shop. I asked him if I could have an ice cream sundae. Instead of putting it in the bowl he got some wet cream and poured it over my head. He got a whole bottle of sauce and poured it on me.

Liam Letters (8)

St John's RC Primary School, Banbury

THE SURPRISE

In the room, there was a rocking chair and the clock struck ten. The rocking chair was scary. The rocking chair was rocking and nobody was there. Lauren heard a scream. There was a knock at the door. It was ten o'clock in the morning.

Kareena Buttler Hawtin (9)

St John's RC Primary School, Banbury

EMILY'S DREAM

It was a mighty, powerful snigger in the dark, creepy room. It sounded like an angry witch. The frightening figure trudged out of the corridor with blood dripping down its red mouth. It came plodding towards me. I was terrified. I couldn't escape ... But it was only a dream.

Stephanie Napierkowski (9)

St John's RC Primary School, Banbury

A MONSTER'S MINI SAGA

John stumbled through a wood full of trees, all around him he could hear moaning, and suddenly a monster jumped out of nowhere and sank its fangs into John's neck, draining all the blood from his body. Suddenly it all went silent and dark. The movie was over!

Jules Aplin (10)

St Mary's School, Henley on Thames

THE ALTERNATIVE GOLDILOCKS

One dark and stormy night, three bears sat in a cave. One said to the other, 'Tell us a story.'
'This is how the story began ...'
'Wait, scrap that,' said another, 'Let's go see the girl in town.'
'Yeah,' exclaimed the third. So they went and ate porridge with her.

Bede Lunn (11)

St Mary's School, Henley on Thames

THE BATTLE

This was going to be my toughest battle yet. I was alone in front of my army, facing thousands of soldiers with their shields held high. I was sweating and my heart pounded. The bugle sounded to charge, 'Turn the computer off, it is time for bed,' said Mum.

Alex Martinez (10)

St Mary's School, Henley on Thames

FIRE FRIGHT!

Catrin closed her front door and saw a huge fire rising above her neighbour's house - wisps of ghostly smoke over the torchlight of flames. She ran inside and dialled 999, then scampered across the road. She was met by an excited neighbour. 'Catrin! you've come for the bonfire party!'

Iwan Stone (10)

St Mary's School, Henley on Thames

A MURDER MYSTERY

The door broke down followed by what appeared to be four CIA agents. What met their eyes was me holding a bloodied knife, crouching over a corpse. The CIA agents, thinking I'd killed the man, looked at me in horror. It was plain to see, I was their chief suspect.

Gabriel Senior (11)

St Mary's School, Henley on Thames

THE STRANGER

Ding dong. Jim walked to the door and opened it. 'Hi, who are you?'
'I am the stranger,' Jim was petrified. He darted upstairs and leaped into the closet. Jim shuffled and turned around. Staring coldly at him was the stranger.
'You've won a TV.' Cheered the stranger.

Marc Emanuel (10)

St Mary's School, Henley on Thames

MINI SAGA MONSTER

Have you ever seen a gruesome monster? I was on my way home from school and a sickly smell met me in the path. It smelled of egg and sewage. Suddenly, a zombie-like creature grabbed me, its skin rotting and a bloody face. My vision went black.

Leo Brandis (11)

St Mary's School, Henley on Thames

THE GHOST

I arrived home late from school on Monday. The house was empty and dark. Suddenly, a light appeared on the wall in front of me. It was a ghost, I thought. I was so scared, I started shaking but then it disappeared, phew! It was Lucy playing with the torch.

Georgia Boyle (10)

St Mary's School, Henley on Thames

CAPSIZE PRACTICE

So there I was, on a frosty morning, at rowing. I got into the boat, I paddled out, I shut my eyes, I threw away my oars, tipped up my boat and *splash!* I quickly swam to shore wet and cold. Never before did my dry clothes feel so good!

Georgina Robinson Ranger (10)

St Mary's School, Henley on Thames

THE TIME MACHINE

Bob stepped into the time machine. Five minutes later he looked out of the window. 'Wow,' he breathed. It really worked! Bob stepped out. He walked into a cave. Suddenly he heard a roar. It was a dinosaur! Bob jumped into the time machine. 'Bob wake up, you'll be late.'

Johnny Lloyd (10)

St Mary's School, Henley on Thames

SANTA HITS A HURDLE

'Ho, ho, ho,' laughed Santa, as he flew towards Australia. It was Christmas Eve and Santa was busy. It was a fine evening but dark, and Rudolph's nose was out of power. What Santa didn't know was his reindeer had fallen asleep. *Crash!* He had hit Ulura ... 'Oh Rudolph.'

Kathryn Craig (10)

St Mary's School, Henley on Thames

NIGHTMARE!

Who was there? Why were they there? What would they want from a seven-year-old boy? What would they do to me? Were they going to bite me? Were they going to grab me or were they gong to take me to some wicked place? Only a nightmare!

Max Barklem (11)

St Mary's School, Henley on Thames

THE CRASH

I was driving along, suddenly, I saw a car and it smashed into another. I didn't know if I would live or not. One of the cars hit my car and I was knocked out for twenty minutes. When I got up, I said, 'That really hurt!'

Harry Green (9)

St Mary's School, Henley on Thames

SUSPICIOUS MINDS

As Elenor turned the key of her house, she heard a bang on the floor. *What could that be?* Elenor thought. She walked into her living room and found a man wearing a mask. 'Hello, who are you?' Elenor quivered.
'It's me, I'm just changing the lights,' her father replied.

Ema Pasic (10)

St Peter's CE Primary School, London

THE FOOTBALL MATCH

As Harry walked down to the football pitch he saw the Liverpool first team coach pull up outside the stadium. Harry ran up to the coach and got out his autograph book. After the match finished Harry was very happy, his team won. He went home holding his autograph book.

Yaqub Abdi (10)

St Peter's CE Primary School, London

GOOD BAUBLES GONE BAD!

There once was a Christmas tree with loads of good baubles. One day, the baubles came to life and turned evil. They turned evil because they wanted to take over the world. So they did. Fortunately, Santa heard the news, so he got into his sleigh and saved the world!

Ellie Silva (11)

St Peter's CE Primary School, London

THE SHOP

Looking around the ancient shop, a tall man opened his briefcase and took out a brown envelope. He left it on a wooden desk and silently walked out. All of a sudden, he collapsed. Strangely, his eyes were opening and closing. The police eventually came but the body had vanished ...

Nina Khan (10)

St Peter's CE Primary School, London

WRONG INTERPRETATION

Susie Salmon rang the doorbell of the house. Nobody answered, so she turned away, when suddenly the door creaked open. Slowly, Suzie walked back until she was confronted by a tall dark figure holding a knife. Then he came into the light clutching a Christmas cracker and exclaimed, 'Merry Christmas!'

Luka Ward (11)

St Peter's CE Primary School, London

DRAGONUV

Once there lived a petrifying dragon called Dragonuv inside a small village. The dragon was on a hunt just for the king and strangely not the whole village. The king called Herod ordered the army to go and shoot Dragonuv at once. So the army sadly shot Dragonuv's heart, terrible.

Zakaria Nabil (10)

St Peter's CE Primary School, London

HOWL!

I was running through the forest as fast as I could. My legs were being scraped by the brambles, the full moon above. My grey hair was getting scruffed up. I was bleeding from multiple places. It was damp and foggy. I rushed into the open. My prey ahead. Howl! ...

Kirk Thompson (10)

St Peter's CE Primary School, London

THE BEGINNING
OF THE END

Selena woke up and walked into the room and stood there waiting. Father said she would go to war with the Clawclan. She went to the forest and saw them stepping closer. A twig snapped. Their heads spun. They growled and walked towards her. She was never ever seen again.

Caitlin Moses (10)

St Peter's CE Primary School, London

BIRTHDAY

On the first of October, it was Jamie's birthday. The doorbell rang. Jamie opened the door. It was his parents. They had a lovely night. They had lots of fun and had lots of stuff to eat. Sadly it was over. They went to bed and lived happily ever after.

Kaan Guney (11)

St Peter's CE Primary School, London

A SCARY HALLOWEEN

One Halloween evening, a young boy called Harry, was going trick or treating. Time soon went by. Harry's mum shouted at him, 'Don't knock at door 27.' Harry, being very foolish, knocked at door 27 without thinking. A white ghost pulled the creaking door open and whispered, 'I've been waiting.'

Louise Brown (10)

School of St Helen & St Katharine, Abingdon

ESCAPE FROM VIENNA

The Great War had trapped Leonie's family as it had trapped most Jews. The only possible escape was over the mountains into Switzerland. Wearing loden capes, they left. Fortunately, they went undiscovered. As Leonie gazed back at Vienna, she thought of those still in danger and prayed for their lives.

Ella Greening (10)

School of St Helen & St Katharine, Abingdon

STUPID ROSS

Ross was a stupid boy, he never believed in curses. That's how Ross died. Ross threw a stone at the haunted grave. Evil Death was furious, Ross had no chance. Evil Death rose and whispered to Ross. Nobody knows what Death said but Ross was cursed. Suddenly, bye, bye Ross.

Eleanor Stubley (10)

School of St Helen & St Katharine, Abingdon

BABY TERROR

Mick found an egg. 'We should take it home and care for it,' suggested Roger.
One day, Mick cried, 'The egg - it's cracking!'
Over the next week, the boys checked the egg 20 times a day, until ...'it's hatching!' yelled Roger.
An hour later, beside the egg, appeared ... A dragon.

Eleanor Butler (9)

School of St Helen & St Katharine, Abingdon

THE STORYTELLER AND THE JOKE TELLER

There once was a storyteller and a joke teller. Both entered a competition, but the storyteller had to tell a joke and the joke teller had to tell a story! Both men felt really silly! They'd entered each other's competitions! But there were more the next day. They both won!

Charlotte Smith (9)

School of St Helen & St Katharine, Abingdon

BY NIGHT

I couldn't sleep. I was terrified. I lay awake listening to the ticking of the clock. Something creaked. I remember tiptoeing onto the landing. The thing was definitely dead. My heart stopped. It gave me a glassy-eyed stare. I shuddered ... and it vanished. I never did venture out again.

Charlotte Hearn (9)

School of St Helen & St Katharine, Abingdon

A FLASH OF COLOUR

I was battling the great waves of the Cornish sea when I glimpsed a quick flash of bright colours. I thought it was a stunning tail. Afterwards I saw a swish of golden hair. It was only after getting off the boat I realised what I had seen that day ...

Lucy Conway (10)

School of St Helen & St Katharine, Abingdon

THE MYSTERIOUS MAN

I hopped on the train, my bag on my shoulder. Everything was fine. I went to the bathroom but left my bag behind. When I got back everything went black. I felt a tap on my head. No one. That's when the train went bang! Life was never the same.

Charlotte Yates (9)

School of St Helen & St Katharine, Abingdon

POOR MRS LADYBIRD!

One bright summer morning Mr Hummingbird was humming his favourite 'Beetles' tune when he heard an awkward *splat* from the nearby hedge. He flew over to inspect. Mrs Ladybird was lying flat on her chubby face not even breathing! Mr Hummingbird rushed her to hospital. She was never seen again!

Louisa Canlan-Shaw (9)

School of St Helen & St Katharine, Abingdon

LOST IN THE WOODS!

The Brownies walked on through the spooky forest, trying to find the clearing. After a while, they noticed a path they had not spotted before. 'This must be it!' shouted the sixer. Unfortunately, they were back where they began. They were lost again. I wonder if anyone found them!

Jemima Matthews (10)

School of St Helen & St Katharine, Abingdon

THE FIGURE

In bed, I shivered from the cool breeze outside. Standing up, creeping towards the window, I heard a faint screaming sound. It seemed to be coming from somewhere near. *Stomp, stomp!* came suddenly from the stairs. *Creak, creak,* came from the landing. It was a dark, dreary figure. I screamed ...

Lara Hull (9)

School of St Helen & St Katharine, Abingdon

BAD DAY AT THE ZOO

One rainy day, two little boys went to the zoo. When they got there, they saw leopards, tigers, lions and elephants. Something bad happened! The leopard escaped from his cage. The leopard was creeping behind Jack and Aiden. He chased Jack and Aiden all around the zoo. They got eaten.

Jack Newberry (7)

Summerfield School, Milton Keynes

THE SCARY DRAGON

On Christmas Day Max was singing a good Christmas song. Suddenly he heard a loud knock on the front door. It was a fierce dragon. He looked very hungry and he had sharp teeth. 'There's no need to worry,' growled the dragon. 'It's only a costume. Do you want chips?'

Bakitharan Vilvarajah (7)

Summerfield School, Milton Keynes

THE SCARY DRAGON

On Christmas Day, Max was singing a good Christmas song. Suddenly, he heard a loud knock on the front door. It was a fierce dragon. He looked very hungry and he had sharp teeth. 'There's no need to worry,' growled the dragon. 'It's only a costume. Do you want chips?'

James Harman (7)

Summerfield School, Milton Keynes

UNTITLED

Buzz was on his spaceship. There was a smash in his window. He nearly flew out the window of his spaceship. Buzz jumped onto Woody's spaceship and both of their spaceships fell down, down to Planet Mars. His alien friends saved them from dying and they woke up fine.

Jack Moran (7)

Summerfield School, Milton Keynes

THE SPOOKY GRUDGE STORY

When the sun drops down and the moon comes up, there lives a thing called the Grudge. When you're still awake, you can hear a suspicious noise coming from your cupboard! It might be the Grudge.
Before the Grudge could eat him, a man switched on the light, it vanished.

Elliott Sutton (7)

Summerfield School, Milton Keynes

UNTITLED

One creepy day there was a girl called Ellie. There was a creepy knock on the door so she opened the door. A nose peeped in the door. It was a horrible witch. Ellie had some salt and put it on the witch. She melted!

Ellie-Mai Moran (7)

Summerfield School, Milton Keynes

VIOLET

One day, there was a mermaid called Violet. She heard a familiar sound. She knew that noise - it was her sister Lizzie. She went to see Lizzie. They went on sea horses. They had so much fun riding on their sea horses.

Samantha Chirapura & Emma Rolfe (7)

Summerfield School, Milton Keynes

SANTA'S BAD NIGHT

One dark night, Santa was flying down with flakes and sparkles to a house. Suddenly he got stuck in the snowy tree! Some wonderful angels with gold sparkly wings got him out of the tree. In the morning, the children were very happy to see Santa in the living room!

Madeleine Beckett (7) & Vicky

Summerfield School, Milton Keynes

CINDERELLA SAGA

Scrub, scrub, scrub. 'Yes Godmother.'
An invitation came through the letter box.
'Cinderella shouldn't go.'
'Please?'
'No.'
But Cinderella did. She danced all night with the prince. She needed to go, she left her slipper behind. The prince demanded to find her and he did. They lived happily ever after.

Tayler Stevenson & Rachel Cochrane (10)

The Globe Primary School, Lancing

FIREWORK NIGHT!

I was in my cosy bed, when I heard a loud bang. What was it? I peered out the window to see a magical explosion sparkle in the sky. I rushed downstairs and saw a glittery line rise to the air. 'Surprise!' called my family, 'Happy firework night!'

Ellie Newton (11)

The Globe Primary School, Lancing

CHRISTMAS!

It was the night before Christmas, when I woke from the sound of bells. I hopped out of bed and saw Santa Claus falling down the chimney with soot on his boots and hiding presents under the tree. He ate all the cookies, and snuck back up the sooty chimney!

Talia Van Houghton

The Globe Primary School, Lancing

THE MAN AT THE DOOR

There was a knock at the door. 'Shannon I'm at your door.'
'Go away.'
Ring, ring, ring.
'Hello?'
'Lauren help me, there is a strange man at the door. His voice is like rocks crumbling.' *Crash!* The door broke down. The strange man killed Shannon by chopping off her head.

Morran Gibbs (11)

The Globe Primary School, Lancing

MYSTERY MAN!

Knock, knock 'Who's there?' I said, nervously.
'Someone you don't know.'
'What do you want?'
'Your soul.'
'Argh! I've got a water pistol and I'm not afraid to use it!'
'Well you can't kill me because I'm a demon.'
'Alright, I will use it.'
Squirt, squirt! 'Oh no!'

Charlie Booth

The Globe Primary School, Lancing

PATCH GOES TO THE PARK

One day, Patch got up and had breakfast. Then he went to the park with his best friend Spot. They went on the swings and the slide. Then it was time for lunch. They ate jam sandwiches and chocolate cake. After lunch they both went home to see their parents.

Max Slater (10)

The Globe Primary School, Lancing

CHRISTMAS

It was Christmas night and I heard a noise. It was the bells ringing. I hopped out of bed and went downstairs. When I got down the creepy stairs, I saw Santa stuck in the chimney with a big bag of toys. He put them under the tree.

Ryan Woollard (10)

The Globe Primary School, Lancing

ROMEO AND JULIET SAGA

Romeo and Juliet loved and cherished each other. Their families battled everyday but that didn't bother Romeo and Juliet, they got married secretly. They died a horrible death at moonlight and that night the families never battled again.

Jamie Frankling (11)

The Globe Primary School, Lancing

HALLOWEEN

I was on the street a lot but not tonight. Monsters, myths and legends ran to my doorstep, knocking and shouting. 'Help!' It's the same night every year. They shouted 'Sweeties! We want some!'
I shouted 'Have some sweets,' and ran to my room, throwing all of them outside.

Stephen Moss (10)

The Globe Primary School, Lancing

WEIRD MAN JIM

Last night was very weird. Hmm. This man called Jim asked some really weird questions. He asked if I put my laptop mouse in a cage so my cat didn't eat it. The next night, I had a dream that my cat ate my laptop mouse. It was very weird.

Ben Watkins (11)

The Globe Primary School, Lancing

THE THREE NASTY PIGLETS AND THE WOLF

There once was a harmless wolf, but three nasty piglets had a plan to get rid of the wolf. Those piglets got a crane and they knocked down the wolf's house whilst the wolf was in the house. There were millions of bricks scattered around. That wolf died.

Harry Lay

The Globe Primary School, Lancing

THE CREAK

Creak! Lewis opened the door. It was pitch-black in the abandoned house. *Creak!* Something was moving upstairs. 'Who's there?' whimpered Lewis. Lewis went up the dusty stairs. There was a black door and an eye was poking out of the doorknob, staring at him.

Jake Richards

The Globe Primary School, Lancing

UNTITLED

In a shallow pool, the mermaid flapped her tail from side to side. Shocked people on the beach saw the mermaid. One of the children pointed. 'There's a mermaid over there!' suddenly a witch appeared out of nowhere and gave her a potion. As she drank it she became human.

Chloe Brooker (11)

The Globe Primary School, Lancing

MR ALIEN VISITS EARTH

Mr Alien lives on the moon. But one day, when he was visiting Earth ... 'Argh!' he suddenly screamed. He had crashed into the Prime Minister's house. Suddenly, the Prime Minister came out and had a party. He said, 'Oh thank you, I hated the house anyway!'

Meghan Murphy (10)

The Globe Primary School, Lancing

JAKE RICHARDS AND THE MAZE

Once, there was a boy called Jake Richards, he was ten. There was a maze; nobody was allowed to go in, unless you gave a toy. Jake got fed up with the system, so he found the guy who owned the maze, and Jake killed him. 'Mission accomplished,' said Jake.

Lewis Foord (10)

The Globe Primary School, Lancing

TOM'S GREAT ADVENTURE

One day, a boy named Tom ran out the shop and went home to do chores for money to get a bass guitar. Tom went back to the shop. On the way, he met talking rabbits. The boss was called Sonic. Then they were in a battle and they won.

Tom Carr (10)

The Globe Primary School, Lancing

FLASH DISAPPEARANCE!

At playtime, it rained. Great, just, great. Then a thunder clap, a lightning flash, and the playing children were gone. 'Guys?' I called, hoping it was just a joke. But no reply. 'Help!' I screamed, 'Anyone!' Then I woke up. 'Phew!' But it wasn't over … The grey tarmac greeted me.

Madeline O'Meara (10)

The Globe Primary School, Lancing

ALIEN VS ZOMBIES

'In the red corner, is alien Zug; in the green corner, is Zombie Gloabe, 3,2,1, go.'
'I bet money on you Zug,' said Smaddy, the other alien.
'It's a steady start for Gloabe. Zug has just splatted Gloabe with goo. Gloabe has crashed down. The champion is Zug!'

Josh Upton

The Globe Primary School, Lancing

MY MINI SAGA

'Eeyore!' That was the last thing Chris remembered that day. Chris woke up to peering fanged faces. They were grabbing for his flesh. Suddenly, a blazing light hit him and the faces were vapourised. A man stepped out of the light and carried injured Chris away into the light …

Tayla Farrell (10)

The Globe Primary School, Lancing

UNTITLED

James, Jayden and Macy were watching when an alien jumped out of the telly. He grabbed Jayden by the throat and dragged him back into the telly. Horrified, the other two followed them. They looked around. 'There's Jayden,' they shouted!
'There's the release button, push it!'

'Run!' they escaped.

Nicholas-Paul Dicks

The Globe Primary School, Lancing

THE MERMAID RESCUE

One day, there was a mermaid and then an eagle swooped down and grabbed her. Then the knight saw the eagle and the mermaid. He went to the castle and ran up the stairs. There, he saw the mermaid and took her back to the sea.

Aisha Cantrill (10)

The Globe Primary School, Lancing

UNTITLED

There was a baby called Harry Potter. There was something special about him. His parents were killed by someone called Voldemort, who was so evil you were not allowed to say his name. He tried to kill Harry Potter but did not have enough power.
The fight goes on!

Jade Preston (11)

The Globe Primary School, Lancing

LITTLE LILLY AND THE DARK HOUSE

Little Lilly ran into her house and slammed the door shut. The house was pitch-black with one candle lit on the hallway floor. Little Lilly crept up to the candle and touched it. She flung back. Suddenly a big angry wolf rampaged out of the cupboard and gobbled her up whole!

James Hicks (10)

The Globe Primary School, Lancing

THE PANDA AND THE FLOWER

'It's morning already? Wow I must have slept in.' Pandi got down from her tree of leaves. When Pandi got down, the field was covered in flowers. But there was one flower that she loved so much. She tucked the flower behind her ear and smiled.

Paige Heasman (10)

The Globe Primary School, Lancing

THE BIG BATTLE

Suddenly, the giant commander dragon shot out of the volcano. The giant Le Ogonedo flew out of the forest. The beast scratched commando and punched him into the town. Le Ogonedo flew down to hit commando. Commando dodged it. *Bam!* Le Ogonedo lay in the town, dead.

Charlie Ellarby (10)

The Globe Primary School, Lancing

BAMBOO

Fluf snuck into the kitchen and she found a note: 'Dear Fluf, there is no cake. There is bamboo and I gave your room a makeover.' Fluf ran into her bedroom. 'Argh!' It's full of bamboo! I wish the panda never moved in.'

Amber Hall (10)

The Globe Primary School, Lancing

THE HAUNTED HOUSE

Mac went into the house. The floor cracked and creaked. He saw something shining in the corner. It was jewels! He picked them up. He tripped over. He got back up, he went outside and he became a billionaire.

Lewis Heavens (10)

The Globe Primary School, Lancing

AMELIA'S DREAM

Amelia lay asleep in bed, all calm and still until she heard the noise that couldn't be real. 'What was that?' murmured Amelia. The wind was whistling, shadows were appearing, and the door slammed shut in a flash. *It must just be a silly dream*! Thought Amelia, but was it?

Casey Morgan (11)
The Globe Primary School, Lancing

THE FASHION POLICE

Hi I'm the fashion police and here is the worst crime ever. Lady GaGa wearing a meat dress. 'Steak, gammon, ugh!' I said.
'Oh hello officer,' said GaGa.
'I'm going to have to give you a ticket.'
'No.'
'£360 by Wednesday.'
'Why officer?'
'Never wear a meat dress again.' Busted.

Cara-Louise Kennedy
The Globe Primary School, Lancing

DELIVERY FOOD MONSTERS

The lights flickered off. It was just me and the pizza man. A pizza man with fur. *fur!* And a McDonald's take out guy with fangs. *fangs!* And a Chinese food man with three legs. Three *legs!* Suddenly I wasn't so hungry anymore …

Bethany Cheung (11)

The Globe Primary School, Lancing

SANDY I'M HERE

'Sandy I'm in your house.' Sandy thought it was her brother. It got closer. 'Sandy I'm at your first step … Sandy I'm at your second step … Sandy I'm at your door, your bedroom door …' Then Sandy was gone.

Lauren Borrill

The Globe Primary School, Lancing

BATTLE!

My friend and I were watching our pets fight. I'd been training my scorpion for weeks. It slashed at his tarantula. It pounced but missed. My scorpion attacked with its red tail and drove the tarantula into the dust. My strong scorpion won the battle against the fierce terrifying tarantula!

Maxwell Goodling (7)

Wetherby School, Notting Hill

BURIED TREASURE

My name is Tom. It was a boiling hot day. I was on a mission to find a treasure map. I saw a cross and started to dig. Hooray! I found the ancient treasure. I was no longer poor, I was rich. I went to live in a beautiful castle.

Harry Murray (7)

Wetherby School, Notting Hill

STORM AT SEA

My friend and I were at sea. Suddenly I saw a pirate ship! It was speeding towards me. We were sailing away. They jumped on the boat! We were diving in the water. Finally I saw a rescue ship heading towards me and my friend. We were safe at last.

Somerset Fell (7)

Wetherby School, Notting Hill

THE SURFING HOLIDAY

It was the first day of the holiday. I zoomed to the beach. When I got there, I grabbed a surfboard and went surfing. It was bit far so I tried to turn around but I fell. I shouted for help. The lifeguard rushed to me. I was saved!

Oliver Crapanzano (7)

Wetherby School, Notting Hill

THE HUMPBACK LANE

I was at the beach and saw a humpback whale. It was very dry. I tried to help; it was too heavy I got a bulldozer to put it in the water. Finally, I got it in the water. He was free!

Jacob Lee (7)

Wetherby School, Notting Hill

THE HUGE EAGLE

'Arghhhh!' The huge eagle picked me up and took me to his nest. Afterwards he tried to eat me but I didn't let him. So I stabbed him and he died. Then I opened my parachute and flew down to a castle and told them the eagle had been killed.

Karam Dhillon (7)

Wetherby School, Notting Hill

THE DIAMOND

America 1942; at that time diamonds were found all over the country but there was one that was priceless and that was the one for me! I set off. I leapt acrobatically onto the roof. Five hours later I'd stolen the sparkling diamond, and then I melted it.

Harry de Montfort (7)

Wetherby School, Notting Hill

THE MONSTER

I was going for a stroll out at night. Something was in the bushes. Suddenly, some ugly thing came out and it was a monster with the great jaws of a dinosaur. I ran into the bush and then it went past me. I went home. I called the cops.

Charlie White (8)

Wetherby School, Notting Hill

THE GINORMOUS MONSTER

The ginormous monster flew across the land. It spat out fire at you. It burned half a city. 'Arghhhhh! We are doomed.' Suddenly, a man threw a sharp sword at him. The monster fell down to the ground into the blazing fire. The fire trucks came, saved the burning city.

Tyler Merriman (7)

Wetherby School, Notting Hill

UNTITLED

'Ahoy! Clean the deck!' chanted Captain Blackbeard. A few minutes later, Captain Blackbeard discovered a black diary. He snatched the diary and walked into his cabin. Just when he got in the middle, a whale bashed into the ship. He fired the cannons and it sank into the water!

David Mariani (7)

Wetherby School, Notting Hill

THE GIGANTIC EAGLE

Have you been standing in front of a 50 foot eagle with only a sword? Well I have! Suddenly he charged! I dodged; he pushed me off the cliff. I fell down and down and down and a rock scraped me. My shirt was ripped and torn. I was bleeding.

Arthur Dobbs (8)

Wetherby School, Notting Hill

THE GHOSTLY BOAT

'Go, go, go!' shouted the Captain and we all rushed into the ship. Suddenly, someone cut the rope attached to the ship and we set sail. It was lovely; I could feel the wind on my soft skin. Every second it got mistier and then I saw the ghostly boat …

Zachary Lennard (7)

Wetherby School, Notting Hill

SNORKELLING

I went on a motor boat. It was a hot sunny day; I was going to France. On the way, I went snorkelling in the middle of the ocean. I could feel the soft seaweed brushing my feet, when suddenly, my snorkel came off, so I went for air.

Rufus Hunter (7)

Wetherby School, Notting Hill

THE BASILISK

One bright day, everyone was playing in the park. Suddenly, an oversized snake turned up and froze half the people there. They were turned to stone. So I called the troop and they took good care of that oversized snake.

Max Teoh (7)

Wetherby School, Notting Hill

THE SCARY GHOST

I woke up to the sound of laughing. My heart was beating so fast, lights were going on and off and the laughing was still going on. I walked along the corridor. I looked around the bendy corner and tripped over a silver wire, *boom!* The ghost had captured me.

Fergus Prest (7)
Wetherby School, Notting Hill

THE SPACE JOURNEY

5, 4, 3, 2, 1, blast off! The jets fired - we were off. 'Woohoo!' My crew shouted. We were getting further and further away from Earth and closer to the Moon. By the time we were halfway to the moon, I had a problem. We were almost out of gas ...

Cy Busson (7)
Wetherby School, Notting Hill

THE HAUNTED HOUSE

As I walked upstairs, the floorboards creaked with every step I took. I entered the room. The glistening, mysterious box sat in the middle. Suddenly, a ghost popped out. I quickly jumped back into the box to get away from the ghost. *Bang!* The ghost was trying to get me.

Alexander Grundy (8)

Wetherby School, Notting Hill

THE JUNGLE

I was in the middle of the Amazon Rainforest, looking for dangerous snakes. But right in the bush, looking down at me, was a snake. Suddenly it struck. Luckily I managed to run away. I reminded myself never to mess with dangerous snakes again. But I would be famous finally!

Alex Morrison (7)

Wetherby School, Notting Hill

CAPTAIN BLACKBEARD

One gloomy day Captain Blackbeard and his crew were on The Falcon, their ship. They were going to Skull Island to get treasure. They got there and there was a dragon! Captain Blackbeard snatched the treasure and went away.

Michael Cash (7)

Wetherby School, Notting Hill

SKULL TEMPLE

I found myself staring into red, bloody eyes. I ran round the temple six times. Then I found a room. I went into the room. Suddenly, the old creaky walls closed in on me. The walls sucked my body in. I was turned into a zombie.

Lucas Mayhew (7)

Wetherby School, Notting Hill

TOADSTOOL TEMPLE

I marched up the stone steps and into a dusty temple. There was a towering statue with a carved mermaid on it. Suddenly, I heard a bang and turned around. I fell over in amazement. The mermaid on the statue was alive and had cast a magical spell on me ...

James Porter (8)

Wetherby School, Notting Hill

CHRISTMAS EVE

It was Christmas Eve and I was snoozing. I heard a distant rumbling. I looked up and saw Santa coming down the chimney. Then he stopped. I saw him stuck in the chimney! Was he going to get out safely? But how?

William Garside (7)

Wetherby School, Notting Hill

PIXIE PATHS

I was sprinting down the dusty Pixie Paths, when I stumbled dramatically. I was lying in front of a small, green, evil pixie. It took me to a dark, sloppy dungeon. Ghosts were wavering creepily around me. I jumped at the greasy metal bars of the cage and fell.

Hugo Rhys Williams (7)

Wetherby School, Notting Hill

MYSTERIOUS TREMORS

Ever since my dad went to Indonesia and died, mysterious tremors had hit his grave. My adventurous uncle took me to my family grave. I had a spooky feeling about my dad and the 80th tremor struck. I was doomed and cursed. I fell to the ground powerless, unconscious and pale.

William James (7)

Wetherby School, Notting Hill

AFRICAN ADVENTURE

The next thing I knew I was on the edge of an African ghost land. A fierce tiger came pounding towards me with a famished lion. They tried to strike me with their claws but I dodged. After a while I lost my energy and I fell unconscious and was gobbled...

Anthony Saidenberg (7)
Wetherby School, Notting Hill

ANIMAL PATH

I stepped into the green jungle and onto a hidden pixie path where fairies lived. The fairies were like tiny, lumpy, spotty insects. A fairy needed me to see if I was a threat with weapons. I had a sharp, pointy, jagged knife. A fairy snatched it from my pocket.

Maxmilian Polley (8)
Wetherby School, Notting Hill

MYSTICAL MOORS

I climbed slowly and carefully out of my camping tent. White fog glided slowly over to me, past the mountains. A ghost rose quickly out the mist. I ran speedily into the dark marshes. It was dancing round me. I said, 'Come with me. I will tell you a secret.'

Jasper Oakley (7)
Wetherby School, Notting Hill

TOADSTOOL TEMPLE

'There are only ruined castles!' Zac cried. 'It's as deserted as an island.' Zac jumped. There was an evil fairy that had a wand which could poison you. Suddenly the fairy pointed her wand towards Zac. He cried, 'Argh!' and tried to avoid her wicked spell but he was dead.

Maxie Clowes
Wetherby School, Notting Hill

PIXIE PATH MYTHS AND LEGENDS

There were many pixies in the twisted tree. This tree was called Evil Tree. There were loads of fights between the pixies and no one knew why. One day the queen was secretly killed but no one knew how or why, except that it was magic.

Hugo Winter (7)

Wetherby School, Notting Hill

MYSTERIOUS PIXIE PATHS

Tom lumbered out of his tent onto the creepy pixie paths. His friend had been kidnapped by evil and petrifying pixies which were like tiny terrifying ants. He needed help! Suddenly Tom heard a shriek from the wilderness. 'Is it too late to save my friend?' he whispered to himself.

Charlie Pliner (7)

Wetherby School, Notting Hill

STRANGE NOISES

Strange noises were coming my way in the middle of the night. I didn't know where the howling noises were coming from. I suddenly saw it. It was a strange man coughing. I thought, *poor him*. When all of a sudden he ran as quickly as a cheetah at me …

Luca Harcombe (7)

Wetherby School, Notting Hill

THE KING'S TEMPLE

The trees whispered in the wind. I saw the towering building made of purple dotted mushrooms, like a Buddhist temple. I heaved myself through the window in the temple. My muscled arms with all my strength approached the king viciously like a salamander on fire. I screamed.

Jack Lonergan (7)

Wetherby School, Notting Hill

THE WILDMAN

I was on a wild wander on The Mystical Moor when I heard a very peculiar bubbling. It was the legendary ghost. Suddenly arms smothered in mud punched with fists of fury, crushing the trees. A huge figure towered over me with eyes like suns and hair like ice ...

Oliver Rose (8)

Wetherby School, Notting Hill

EXCITING ADVENTURE

I wanted an exciting adventure. I was striding along the rocky path when there was a sudden loud rumbling noise. I started running as fast as possible. I felt like an Olympic runner at full speed. I suddenly heard a truck. This was my chance to leave. I took it!

Nicholas Douglas-Home (8)

Wetherby School, Notting Hill

MYSTICAL ADVENTURES

James stepped out of his time machine. He was in a massive, towering colosseum. The sound was deafening. Gladiators were fighting ferociously, sword to sword, and a swing of a sharp, shiny axe. He let go of the axe. James ducked but not in time. James' head was chopped off.

David Doughty (8)

Wetherby School, Notting Hill

NEVER TO BE SEEN AGAIN

Bang! I was woken by a loud noise. I peeked outside 'Argh!' I yelled. Trees were tumbling down. I saw a brown ladder. I quickly scampered up it. Suddenly, a huge tree caught my leg, hurling me down into the depths of the world. I was never to be seen again.

William Whiu (8)

Wetherby School, Notting Hill

GHOSTLY HAPPENINGS

It was a magical night, John was sweating. Suddenly he heard a strange buzzing noise. He was in the mystical moors. The buzzing was coming from higher up a chaotic hill. Blackness surrounded him, a luminous glow appeared. Suddenly, a hovering creature was bubbling above him. His last moments.

Nicholas Mallinckrodt (7)

Wetherby School, Notting Hill

THE HADRAGEL

I woke up from being unconscious in a deep pit. I looked up the walls which were slimy and grey. Then I looked up and saw a horrible sight, the Hadragel was staring at me with its giant, red eyes. It swooped down at me. I screamed.

Darius Hagmann-Smith (9)

Wolvercote Primary School, Wolvercote

ODOUR OF THE AIR, POMPEII, SOMETIME AD

The choking, acidic gases whirl over the heads of any man, woman or child close to Mount Vesuvius. Acrid and invisible, it curls around any unlucky living organism, suffocating them like a boa constrictor. The volcano is just visible over the high rooftops, spurting lava and volcanic rock.

Eleanor Ivimey-Parr (9)

Wolvercote Primary School, Wolvercote

SHOPPING

One spring day a teddy bear sat peacefully, twiddling his thumbs. Suddenly a huge, dark shadow loomed over him and two great big hands reached out to grab him. *Oh no, help*! He thought to himself, horrified. 'Can I have that one?' said the little girl pointing to his neighbour.

May Rainbird (8)

Wolvercote Primary School, Wolvercote

THE ICE FAIRIES

As I stood in my garden, listening to the soft tinkling of voices, a mist enveloped me. The cold bit at my fingertips but I was too enthralled to notice. I stood in silence until I froze through. But then I turned away, knowing I would never see them again.

Posy Putnam (10)

Wolvercote Primary School, Wolvercote

THE BIRTHDAY SURPRISE

Clara went to hockey on Saturdays. This Saturday was special. It was her birthday! But she was disappointed, she wasn't having a party. When Clara arrived at hockey, the hall was dark. Where was everyone? Suddenly, people appeared. There were streamers, balloons - a cake! 'Surprise!' everyone yelled. What a party!

Daphne Pleming (8)

Wolvercote Primary School, Wolvercote

SNOWY SURPRISE!

Snowflakes fall softly as I snuggle under the covers. I hear something ... a sound of feet pounding up the stairs. At every step, I pull myself further under the duvet. I wait and listen. My heart misses a beat as the door swings open, and then I see Santa!

Sarah Cox (9)

Wolvercote Primary School, Wolvercote

YOUNG WRITERS
INFORMATION

We hope you have enjoyed reading this book - and that you will continue to enjoy it in the coming years.
If you like reading and creative writing drop us a line, or give us a call, and we'll send you a free information pack.

Alternatively if you would like to order further copies of this book or any of our other titles, then please give us a call or log onto our website at **www.youngwriters.co.uk**

Young Writers Information
Remus House
Coltsfoot Drive
Peterborough
PE2 9BF
Tel: (01733) 890066

Published by
Federation of Family
History Societies
(Publications) Ltd.
Units 15-16
Chesham Industrial Centre
Oram Street, Bury
Lancs BL9 6EN
United Kingdom

Copyright © Lilian Gibbens

ISBN 1-86006-136-2

First published 2001

Printed and bound by
Uniprint

Basic

R

PART 1
Researching
London Ancestors

Lilian Gibbens

SERIES EDITOR
Pauline M. Litton

FEDERATION OF FAMILY HISTORY SOCIETIES

CONTENTS

103312856

INTRODUCTION

Basic Facts About Research in London is divided into two booklets. Part 1, *Researching London Ancestors,* is aimed to help family historians undertake research in London to a satisfactory completion and describes some of the main record offices and a small part of their collections The second booklet *London Repositories,* will supply a brief description of the record offices (and other places of interest to the family historian), together with addresses, telephone numbers, fax numbers, email addresses and websites.

What do we mean by 'London'?

The large area that most family historians now consider to be London is illustrated by *The London Family History Societies' Registration Districts Map,* compiled by Susan Lumas (and published by Society of Genealogists). It covers the modern Greater London area which today contains parts of Essex, Kent, Surrey, Hertfordshire and Middlesex and which, at a stretch, could be said to include the edges of Buckinghamshire. The reader should realise that during the greater part of the nineteenth century, and the early part of the twentieth century, the outer parts of this area were entirely rural. Indeed, some parishes closer to the City of London (the 'real' London) such as Hackney, were fairly rural until the mid-nineteenth century.

It must be remembered that places now considered to be in London were, before the latter part of the nineteenth century, in the various home counties. For example: Islington was in Middlesex, Southwark was in Surrey and Greenwich was in Kent. The term London then meant the City of London. The county of London (and its administrative body - The London County Council [LCC]) was a relatively new creation designed to facilitate administration, especially in respect of education, and the Greater London Council (the GLC) came into existence in 1965. At the tail end of the nineteenth century the parishes surrounding the City grew in population and they developed into Boroughs or Urban District Councils, then Metropolitan Boroughs, eventually becoming absorbed into the huge Greater London Boroughs. To illustrate: the present London Borough of Camden was formerly the Metropolitan Boroughs of St Pancras, Hampstead and Holborn; the London Borough of Barnet comprises the former Metropolitan Boroughs of Barnet, Finchley, Hendon, Friern Barnet Urban District (in Middlesex) and the East Barnet Urban District (which was then in the county of Hertfordshire). In 1965, the City of Westminster also enveloped the Metropolitan Boroughs of Paddington and St Marylebone. To add to the researcher's confusion, the Registration Districts used for both civil registration and census returns changed from time to time. The area covered by the London & North Middlesex Family History Society can be used to illustrate this point. In 1851 and 1861 the districts were Marylebone, Hampstead, St Pancras, Islington, St Giles, Holborn, Clerkenwell, St Luke (Finsbury), London East, London West, London City, Hendon (part), Barnet, and Edmonton (part). In 1871, 1881 and 1891 Clerkenwell and St Luke were absorbed into the Holborn Registration District and London East and London West became part of the London City Registration District.

The main purpose of this booklet is to help you find 'London' ancestors prior to 1900. When the modern bodies of administration did not exist; when on the whole the parish was the device for administering poor law, health and environment and medical services. The problem is, that the records created under the older administrations are to be found in the record offices run by modern bodies. But your so-called ancestors may, in fact, have been Surrey ancestors, or Middlesex ancestors, or Essex ancestors, depending upon the year and location. Today, most 'Londoners' and visitors to the Metropolis consider a place like Barking, Tottenham or Enfield, as part of the great conglomeration. In 1850, Barking was a flourishing - indeed *the* most prominent *fishing* town in England, but it was in the county of Essex. Tottenham was a rural village and Enfield was a quiet, country town in Middlesex, used as a dormitory for the wealthy who needed to have easy access to London, and surrounded by farmland and brickfields. As happened in most places in the Greater London area the changes were brought about by the coming of the railways. When a greater variety of fresh fish could be rapidly and easily brought to London markets by goods trains, from places such as Hull or Brixham, the demand for Barking's fishermen waned. The decline of the fishing industry forced an economic and social change on the Essex town. The changes in Tottenham occurred when the Jewish furniture industries moved out of the East End taking their workers with them to the new estates of cheap housing being erected and bigger and better factories, with the facility to transport their products by road and rail and the New River waterway.

Today, many such places in the G.L. area, which serve as dormitories for the City workers, such as Pinner, Hillingdon, Harrow, Barnet, Enfield etc., still have a 'country town' atmosphere; in fact, 'us locals' don't really consider we live .in London. When we go 'up to London' we usually go to 'the West End' which is mainly in the City of Westminster.

Transitory Ancestors

To further complicate matters, many of our seemingly London ancestors were, in truth, either 'incomers' or those just passing through and this is true going back through the centuries. London, and its surroundings, has always been a place where 'strangers' and 'foreigners' have come to live. In the past the term 'strangers' was applied to those from overseas, and 'foreigners' were those from parishes elsewhere in the United Kingdom. Londoners have always tolerated those speaking other languages and practising other religions (provided they proved to be useful

3

to the community, such as the fourteenth century Flemish weavers and the later Huguenot weavers). Some incomers from overseas lived in London temporarily, passing on to Australia or the USA; some intended to move on, but somehow forgot to go. Others came from the country areas – from Suffolk, Norfolk, Lancashire, Scotland, driven out from their home villages by poor harvests in the period 1830-1850, often mistakenly thinking that London was the place where they would make a fortune, eventually realising it was a place to suffer from impoverishment.

London - a place of many record sources

I've no doubt that many of you have realised that London is a place where many record sources are available, not necessarily restricted to London research. Access to National records is possible, such as the indexes to registered births, marriages and deaths in England and Wales in the rooms of the Registrar General at the Family Records Centre, together with those of Scotland (by computer terminal); Wills after 1858 at First Avenue House; and a cornucopia of record sources at the Public Record Office in Kew, which includes the records of the Metropolitan Police and records of the armed services to name but a few.

RESEARCHING IN LONDON

Coming to London to do family history research

Bearing in mind the complexity inherent in undertaking research in London, the golden rule is: *Always do your homework first!* Before attempting to travel first define the precise purpose of your trip. Are you (a) going to use the sources available to research your ancestry, which may or may not be centred in London itself, but elsewhere in the UK, or (b) are you intending to research London ancestors.

Ask yourself 'Is my journey really necessary?' Will the end result be worth the expenditure of time, effort and money? A little advance thought may prevent a wasted journey and save you money. Ask yourself the following questions:

♦ What information is wanted? Define the problem(s) precisely. Write them down in list form! Can the data you need be gathered from one record type only, or will it be necessary to look at a variety of records? If the latter, can they all be accessed in one place? If the answer to the last question is No then your trip to London must be planned very carefully, especially if you can spend only one day in the Capital.

♦ Where are the records to be found to furnish such data? Can they be accessed nearer to home? - on film at the local LDS Family History Centre, or on microfiche at a local Reference Library, or by computer at your local lending library or Computer Café (to access the International Genealogical Index or the 1881 Census Index)? If you own a microfiche reader (or can use one in, say, the local library) are you able to purchase microfiche of registers (or other records) you wish to read? A set of microfiche may prove cheaper than the railway fare (or coach fare) to London. Can you employ a paid research service provided by a London Local Archive? It may prove to be more economic to do so, and they will have the local expertise at their fingertips. If not, do they maintain a list of local researchers? Is the material available at more than one place in London?

◆ To finalise your plans you may need to write to the relevant record office for guidance, or to purchase their published Guide to Holdings, or you can 'surf the net' for resources. Without full details you cannot plan an efficient day's work. Skip this part, and you may fail to derive the full benefit from your expedition to London.

◆ Why not contact the appropriate family history society? Do they have indexes to purchase, or that may be searched for members or non-members? Do they publish a booklist of local books that can be ordered by post and read prior to your visit? Do they have a scheme for reciprocal research, or a list of researchers?

USING LONDON RECORD OFFICES

'London' record offices can be divided broadly into three groups: those acting as repositories for 'national' records (FRC, PRO), those with custody of material specific to a local area (London Local Archives), and those which house records of a specific nature (First Avenue House for Wills, Lambeth Palace for Church records especially those of the Archbishop of Canterbury, including Wills and Marriage Licences).

Before making your trip find out as much as possible about the record office(s) you intend to visit. What are the opening hours? These may vary from record office to record of office. They may vary from day to day. Check the closing time. Does the office stay open late on particular days? Does the office provide access for disabled readers? What facilities are provided: photocopying, cloakroom, lockers, common rooms in which to eat sandwiches, drinks machines, toilets? Are there facilities for the disabled? Even today there are one or two places where a toilet is not available to the researcher! If you have a weakness, this could be a problem. If you cannot eat in at lunch time, are there any recommended cafes, pubs, eateries or even a park? Will you need to book a seat to use a table, or a film/fiche reader? Is a charge made? What is the advance notice required for orders? Seemingly minor details, but prior knowledge will smooth your way on the day. Working in an archives department the author frequently sees the disappointed faces of people who turn up on 'closed' days only to be turned away; particularly disappointing if the researcher has travelled thousands of miles by air. But, it does illustrate a lack of thoroughness in their approach to work.

Most important of all, check that the office you intend to visit *does hold the records you want to look at!* Some records may be held in other record offices, say County Record Offices, and not the local archives department, especially Ecclesiastical records as these may be sorted by Diocese rather than by London Borough or Parish. An example of this is Cockfosters — although it is within the London Borough of Enfield, the records are held in Hertfordshire County Record Office as the parish falls within the Diocese of St Albans. There is also a possibility that parish records are still in the care of the incumbent, such as those of Staines (until recently, when they passed to the LMA) and St Giles in the Fields which must still be viewed at the church, for a small fee (set by the Church Commissioners each year). If this is the case make sure you ask whether or not you may look at all the records, or search for one entry only? Ask what the fee will be ahead of your visit, to save you embarrassment. Will *you* be able to look at the records, or will someone do it for you while you wait (as at the Chapel of the Savoy)?

When you are sure of all the facts, then book your visit (if it is necessary) by telephone, letter, fax or email to the specific archive repository. This will ensure that you have the use of a machine, a seat, or table, which may be in short supply in small offices, especially in the busy times of the year. Some research rooms have only a few seats and table spaces and only three or four microform readers so it pays to book in advance. Of course, it is not necessary to book when using the Family Records Centre, First Avenue House, the Public Record Office, or Guildhall Library. In certain record offices, such as Lambeth Palace Library, you may be required to take a letter of introduction with you when you first visit.

Thoroughly read any guide to a record office you have not visited before. Most local London Archives publish printed guides to their holdings and may publish them on websites. If you are using the national offices for the first time, make time to read Audrey Collins' *Basic Facts About Using the Family Records Centre,* or *Basic Facts About Using Wills after 1858 and First Avenue House* (both published by the Federation of Family History Societies). Before visiting a Greater London Cemetery or Crematorium Office make sure you browse through *Greater London Cemeteries and Crematoria,* revised edition by Clifford Webb (published by Society of Genealogists) which will tell you where the records are held, what date they begin, and whether or not you are able to make a personal search (in some cases enquiries must be dealt with by post, together with a pre-payment). It may also be useful to read *Basic Facts About Using Record Offices for Family Historians,* by Tom Wood (FFHS).

It is also wise to make a final check with the record office, the day before you visit to make sure that the office will be open on the day. Sudden illness among a small staff may enforce closure of a local record office at short notice. Many have only two or three staff and it is required that one member of staff watches the reading room while another gets out the records from the strong room.

If you lack knowledge of the geographical area in which you intend to research, read the relevant *Victoria County History* (if it has been completed), or the *Survey of London.* Copies of these works are sometimes available in good county reference libraries or through the library lending system (with sufficient prior notice). If you intend to spend more than one day in London, then this can be undertaken at the London Metropolitan Archives or Guildhall Library. In addition, invest in a modern A-Z of London and the appropriate Godfrey facsimile Ordnance Survey Maps (which cover the period from 1863 until 1914) if they have been published for the area.

Last of all, work out your travel arrangements. Will the train times fit into the office hours, leaving you sufficient time to research. Will you need to use train, underground, bus, or can you walk? Remember you can usually ask a bus driver to set you down at the appropriate bus stop, but don't expect all drivers to know their routes - sadly they don't. If using a taxi always ask what the fare is likely to be (having studied a map in advance so that you can demonstrate that you know the way ... a little).

A question often asked is: is the area safe to walk in? On the whole, most places are reasonably safe, even after dark, provided you are fairly street-wise. This applies anywhere in the world. I have heard American visitors say how fearful they were to walk around St Pancras - but is it any worse than some parts of New York, Boston, Washington DC or even Paris? Common sense must prevail. Always study your route in advance so you will not need to brandish large maps. Look determined, don't flaunt a large flashy handbag or shoulder bag, a 'posh' camera, or camcorder; keep your money, keys and travel tickets hidden on your body and only a little money (expendable) in your bag. If forced to ask directions, choose your subject carefully. However, most visitors to London find the inhabitants fairly friendly and helpful.

On the day of your visit ensure that you have available a £1, 50p, 20p and 10p coin − all of these may be needed for lockers (you will get your money back). Many record offices *require* readers to deposit their belongings in a locker. Some may limit the items that can be taken into the reading room. Don't carry your belongings in a huge bag − they may not fit into the locker (some lockers will not take a normal brief case). Take the minimum − only what is necessary. If you are taking documents or copy documents make sure that they carry labels identifying your ownership, or they may be confiscated. It is useful to wear clothing with pockets in which to put small change for photocopies, credit cards, locker keys, hankies etc. One researcher puts all her items in a large jacket pocket, fastening it with an enormous safety pin to foil the pick-pockets in the FRC! Remember to carry *pencils* with you, pens and biros are not usually allowed in record offices (apart from the FRC) because of the danger to the documents.

7

WHAT CAN YOU EXPECT TO FIND

London **Local Records Offices** can provide access to material specific to a local area. You will find that the selection of material varies from office to office. Some may hold microfilm copies or transcripts (sometimes originals) of parish registers and parish records (vestry minutes, churchwardens accounts, poor law records and early rate books), the records — and sometimes registers of members — of nonconformist churches and chapels in the area, perhaps copies of Roman Catholic Records. Most certainly they will have microfilm copies of the census returns from 1841 to 1891 for their area (and sometimes for contiguous areas), and may hold those of the parish returns (known as censuses) for 1811, 1821, and 1831. You may also find indexes to cemeteries, memorial inscriptions in churches and churchyards, local wills, deeds, documents and antiquarian material. If the office is an official repository for records of local administration you may find Borough Council records, ratebooks (from 1900 to 1965 only), Land Tax (1910 Domesday), Electoral Registers and Poll Books as well as local directories, Kelly's Streets and Trades Directories (many will hold microfilm copies of the holdings of directories held at Guildhall), volumes listing street name changes, and plans and orders relating to renumbering of streets in the area. Most offices will house thousands of photographs, prints, drawings, paintings of the area and one or two record offices have computerised maps and drawings to provide easy access and quick copies. Other items may include ordnance survey maps, tithe records and maps, enclosure maps, drainage plans, insurance plans, records for local estates, businesses, and local people. You may, if you are lucky, find undertakers' records, or records relating to the ARP and bomb damage in World War II (together with pictures of the bomb sites). There will be books on the area and its environs. Best of all, Local Newspapers! Now you can see why it is so necessary to obtain the guide to the holdings.

At the **Family Records Centre** you will find microfilm copies of the decennial census returns, Wills in the Prerogative Court of Canterbury (PCC Wills), estate duty records, nonconformist registers (non parochial registers). The various sections of the surname index to the 1881 Census Returns for England and Wales are available on microfiche, along with the National Sort. This index can also be accessed via the computer terminals, with *FamilySearch, Ancestral File* and the *Vital Records Index* (which contains references not included in the International Genealogical Index in *FamilySearch).* You will also find the indexes to registered births, marriages and deaths from July 1837; Marine births and deaths; Army births, marriages and deaths; Naval deaths; RAF deaths; Consular births marriages and deaths; adoptions in England and Wales from 1927 (all on the ground floor); indexes to non-statutory miscellaneous Foreign Registers of births, marriages and deaths.

The **Public Record Office** at Kew houses the 1910 Valuation Records; Tithes; Enclosures; the correspondence of the Poor Law Commissioners with the parishes; records of the Metropolitan Police Force and the armed services; and some cemetery records: the Gibraltar Row burial ground in Bethnal Green, St Thomas Square Cemetery in Hackney, the Royal Hospital Cemetery(Navy) at Greenwich, the Royal Hospital Chelsea (Army) cemetery, with indexes to the registers of Bunhill Fields Burial Ground. You may also find apprenticeship records, tax records, manorial records for the London area and records of the Duchy of Lancaster (which encloses a number of suburban areas) including records of inquests held within the Duchy. You will need to study the published guide to the holdings at Kew before visiting, and obtain the free leaflets, which can also be downloaded from the PRO website. (**www.open.gov.uk/leaflets**)

If searching for a Will in London then you may need to visit the FRC, First Avenue House, Guildhall Library, or London Metropolitan Archives. Copies may be available in local London Records Offices. The London Metropolitan Archives and Guildhall Library both publish leaflets about their holdings of probate documents. If you send a large self-addressed, appropriately stamped envelope, they will post a copy to you.

Apart from Wills, **Guildhall Library,** the Manuscripts section and the map section may provide you with a wealth of material. It is here that you can view on microfilm the records of the numerous city parishes, together with the records of St Leonard Shoreditch and St Andrew Holborn. St Andrew Holborn is a difficult parish, as part of it is within the City of London and part outside. The Library also holds the records of three ecclesiastical courts: the Commissary Court of London, the Archdeaconry Court of London and the Peculiar Court of the Dean and Chapter of St Paul's, which dealt with probate and marriage licences. Sources for tracing apothecaries, physicians, surgeons and midwives can be accessed. You will also find maps (of the City of London, the surrounding parishes and the suburbs such as Pinner), prints, photographs, drawings — many (over 30,000!) digitised and accessed by computer through the Library's *Collage* system, also available on the internet at **http.//collage.nhil.com** Lloyds Marine Collection; City Livery Company Records; records of Christ's College School (the Bluecoat School); the records of the Central Criminal Court. In the library there are copies of London Directories (Boyle's Court Guides, Kelly's Streets & Trades Directories and others), covering a period from 1750 onwards, the Gentleman's Magazine, Boyd's Burials, Boyd's Marriages, the IGI, and a selection of Census Returns for the City of London and its immediate surrounds, such as the Strand. There is also a large collection of register transcriptions (printed or otherwise) for London parishes, non-conformists, Jews and Huguenots. You may find a use for the several cuttings collections and similar material or the plethora of London books available on the open shelves, with professional directories for politicians, actors, lawyers, doctors, surgeons etc., etc., Guildhall Library publishes several guides to their holdings (see reading list at the end of this booklet).

There is also a City of London burial index 1813-1853 compiled by Cliff Webb, John Hanson, Monnica Stevens and others. If you cannot get to use the index at Guildhall Library then parts can be purchased on microfiche through the Society of Genealogists and family history societies. A list giving details of the parishes and dates covered by the *Pallot Index* to marriages, circa 1780-1837, can also be viewed at Guildhall Library; the Pallot index is held by Achievements Ltd in Canterbury. It contains many entries relating to parishes whose records were destroyed during World War II.

The **Corporation of London Records Office** holds records relating to the City of London, Freedom records, inquisitions post mortem 1619-1620; Coroners records (mostly early, but some from 1788-1984 which are being indexed); prison inquests for Southwark 1788-1932 (also being indexed); records of the Court of Sessions of the City of London, records of the Magistrates Courts (Guildhall and Mansion House), and those of the Civic Courts such as the Court of Hustings, Sheriffs and City of London Court, Court of Requests, Court of Orphans; Freemasons returns 1799-1967; Victuallers' Licences 1683-1857; records of the City of London Police Force, City of London School, Freemen's Orphan School, and records of Clubs and societies etc., as well as estate records. A fuller list can be found in *An Introductory Guide to the Corporation of London Records Office* eds. Hugo Deadman and Elizabeth Scudder (published by the Corporation of London).

The **London Metropolitan Archives [LMA** (formerly the Greater London Record Office)] offers the records of the parishes in the present Greater London Area (parish registers, parish records such as vestry minutes, churchwardens accounts, rate books); poor law records (including those of workhouses and schools); Middlesex, London and Surrey Wills; nonconformist records; those of the Coram Foundation (Foundling Hospital); electoral registers; school records of the LCC and others; records of the New River. They hold the original records of parishes such as Hackney, St Marylebone and Paddington and have provided the local offices with microfilm copies. Some of the records are indexed but, unfortunately for us, these indexes are now available only on microfilm and many are very difficult to read. The paper indexes are now to be found in the Society of Genealogists. The Middlesex Deeds Registry is also held at the LMA. Also, the Middlesex Sessions records (Quarter Sessions, Petty Sessions), lists of Roman Catholics and other dissenters, and many, many other items including the records of Tower Hamlets Cemetery. The library shelves house a large number of books on London and the suburbs and there is a big map department and photographic section. The author has visited the LMA for a great many years and has used only a quarter of the records available. The LMA publishes a wide selection of free leaflets and lists of holdings are available to purchase on microfiche.

The **City of Westminster Archives Centre** holds the parish registers and records for the ancient (and some more modern) parishes in the City of Westminster, together with records of nonconformist chapels. Parish records include ratebooks, apprenticeship records, vestry minutes, churchwardens and overseers accounts, grave registers and workhouse and other poor law material. They have custody of the Grosvenor Estate Records (you need permission prior to access), those of Gillow's the furniture makers, and of Messrs. Liberty. There is a selection of Poll Books, electoral registers, local directories, London directories (including Boyle's Court guides, Royal Red Books, Royal Blue Books and Kelly's Streets and Trades Directories). They hold the rate books for St Marylebone and Paddington (only every census year for this parish). There is a cuttings collection, a trades card collection, and material relating to the Theatre along with a vast collection of pamphlets, photographs and prints; material relating to the St John's Wood artists and other artists. Most of the printed material is referenced by a card index, and also a vast deeds collection. There are a few guides to the material held but a thorough browse is always useful.

A useful place for family historians is the **City of Westminster Central Reference Library** in Orange Street, off Leicester Square. Here is housed a selection of Crockfords directories and Clergy Lists, as well as books relating to the Theatre, Cinema and their stars. There is also a section relating to the arts and artists.

Westminster Muniments are housed in Westminster Abbey. Prior appointments are necessary and you can access the records of St Margaret Westminster and St Peter's (Westminster Abbey); there are also lists of the memorial inscriptions to be found in the Abbey.

A visit to the **Society of Genealogists** can help with London research (and research elsewhere in the world). They have a large collection of London books and transcriptions. Here are held indexes to the Inland Revenue Apprenticeship records (1710-1774) held at PRO, Boyd's inhabitants of London, Boyd's Marriages and Boyd's Burials, copies of the Gentleman's Magazine, The London Review, professional directories for politicians, doctors, writers, lawyers, artists etc., school lists and histories, also university registers and histories. There is a vast collection of Birth Briefs supplied by members, a document collection, parish register copies, census returns, and the indexes of GRO births marriages and deaths, as well as those to Wills from First Avenue House. Not to mention the Great Card Collection, the basic text books, the standards works on various counties, and the enormous collection of memorial inscriptions. The society holds a large number of works on CD-Rom which can be viewed by computer and there is access to the internet. You will also find microfilm copies of newspapers and the Surname index to the 1881 Census returns.

The **Catholic Central Library** in Lancing Street, off Eversholt Street, which runs down the side of Euston Station, has transcripts of the registers of many London Roman Catholic Chapels and Missions. Copies are also to be found in the Society of Genealogists.

The **Historical Manuscripts Commission** is housed in Quality Court, off Chancery Lane, and it is here that information relating to manors and parishes can be found as well as the National Register of Archives (NRA). There is also a computerised index to Businesses and indexes to deposited records throughout Britain. Details can be found in the various free leaflets available from the HMC or from their website: **http://www.hmc.gov.uk/main.htm** or from the NRA website at **http://www.hmc.gov.uk/sheets/**

A wealth of material relating to London and to trades unions can be found at the **British Museum.**

The records of the **House of Lords** have been kept at Westminster since 1497 (earlier records are held at the PRO). Material which may interest family historians may include that relating to the employment of staff in the Palace of Westminster, peers, peerage claims, MPs and officials of Parliament, as well as Acts of Parliament (including those relating to divorce and naturalisation), parliamentary diaries, clerks papers and private political papers. A fuller list appears in *Local London Archives,* published by Greater London Archives Network.

The Surrey History Centre in Woking holds the records of **Brookwood Cemetery.** Many London people are buried in this cemetery; there are many burials of parish paupers from the parishes of Bloomsbury, Hackney, and others.

Putting flesh on the bones

The following sites, and others to numerous to mention here, may provide material to flesh out the family histories you are compiling:

The Museum of London, the Office for National Statistics Library in Sloane Square; the House of Lords Record Office, the British Library (Electoral Registers); the British Library (Manuscripts Section); the British Library (Newspaper Library); the Church of England Record Centre; Bethlem Royal Hospital; Great Ormond Street Hospital; Royal London Hospital Archives; BT Archives; Post Office Archives; National Maritime Museum and Records section; National Army Museum; Imperial War Museum; the Royal Institute of British Architects; the Institute of Surveyors; Trinity House; the Institute of Historical Research; Companies House; Wellcome Institute Medical Library; the medical library at Marylebone Library, Friends House (Quaker library); the Geffreye Museum (furniture) in Shoreditch; the Museum of Childhood (London Fields).

A full list of addresses of the record offices mentioned, and others, together with telephone numbers and other details will be published in *Basic Facts about... Research in London, Part 2: Record Repositories.*

SELECTIVE FURTHER READING

Atkins, P. J., *The Directories of London, 1677-1977,* Mansell
Benton, A., *Irregular Marriages in London before 1754,* SoG
Bevan, A., *Tracing your Ancestors in the Public Record Office,* HMSO
Brett-James, N., *The Growth of Stuart London,* George Allen & Unwin
Guildhall Library, *City of London Parish Registers, Greater London Parish Registers; Nonconformist, Roman Catholic, Jewish and Burial Ground Registers,* all published by Guildhall Library Publications
Gandy, Michael, *Catholic Missions and Registers,* Vol I *London & Home Counties*
Georgano, N., *The London Taxi,* Shire Publications
Gibson, Jeremy, *Local Newspapers 1750-1920. England and Wales; Channel Islands; Isle of Man,* FFHS
Gibson, Jeremy, and Creaton, Heather, *Lists of Londoners,* FFHS
Halliday, S., *The Great Stick of London: Sir Joseph Bazalgette and the Cleansing of London,* Sutton Hardback publications
Harvey, R., *Genealogical Sources: Guildhall Library,* Guildhall Library Publications
Herber, Mark, *Clandestine Marriages: in Chapel and Rules of the Fleet Prison 1680-1754 Volume I and Volume II*
Horn, Pamela, *The Victorian Town Child,* Sutton Publishing
Kaye, D., *Old Trolley Buses,* Shire Publications
Knight, R and Yeo, G., *Greater London History Sources, Volume 1: City of London,* Guildhall Library Publications with Greater London Archives *Network, 2000.* It lists the holdings for the City of London, those at Guildhall and at the St Bartholomew's Hospital Archives and Museum. Deals with parishes, City Companies, schools, fairs, markets, clubs, associations etc., and hospitals, Large index at back.
Lewis, Pat, *My ancestor was a Freemason,* SoG
Lumas, S., *Making use of the Census,* PRO Publications
May, T., *Victorian and Edwardian Horse Cabs,* Shire Publications
Melling, J. K., *Discovering London's Guilds and Liveries,* Shire Publications
Public Record Office, *The Family Records Centre: Introduction to Family History,* PRO Publications
McLaughlin, E., *Wills before 1858; The Censuses: 1841 to 1891; Family History from Newspapers,* all from the McLaughlin Genealogical Guides Series
Nissel, Muriel, *People Count,* HMS0
Raymond, Stuart, *London & Middlesex. A Genealogical Bibliography,* (2 vols.) FFHS, Lists standard works such as Lysons London, Victoria County History and hundreds of other printed sources.
Rennison, Nick, *The London Blue Plaque Guide,* Sutton Publishing
Richardson, J., *City of London Past,* Phillimore

13

Scholfield, J., *The building of London: Conquest to the Great Fire*, Museum of London

Humphery -Smith, Cecil, *The Phillimore Atlas & Index of Parish Registers*

Stow, J., *The survey of London*, facsimile, Sutton Publishing

Webb, C., *My ancestors were Londoners; An index of London Schools and their records; London Apprentices Series*, Volumes 1-34; *London's Bawdy Courts Vol 1: 1703 -1713 (Consistory Court of London) Index to cases and depositions*, All published by SoG

West Surrey FHS, *Suburban London before 1837: Map shows parish boundaries; A List of Books and Articles about London & Middlesex Places, including Metropolitan Surrey;* and *Middlesex Contiguous Parishes* (leaflet); *Genealogical research in Late Victorian and Edwardian London; Preliminary Guide to Middlesex Parish Documents; Guide to London & Middlesex Manorial Records; Genealogical Gazetteer of Mid-Victorian London; The Hundreds of Middlesex* (leaflet)

Wittich, J., *Discovering London Street Names*, Shire Publications; *Discovering London's Inns and Taverns*, Shire Publications

Wood, Tom *An Introduction to Civil Registration*, 2nd Edn. 2000, FFHS

Wolfston, P., revised by Webb, C., *Greater London Cemeteries and Crematoria*, SoG

Yeo, Geoffrey, *Record Keeping at St Pauls Cathedral;* Journal of Society of Archivists, Vol. 8 No. 1 1986 pp 30-44, contains references to potential sources.

Aldous, Vivienne E., My ancestors were Freemen in the City of London, SoG

Also see the following topographical works

The A-Z of Georgian London. Introductory notes by Ralph Hyde. London Topographical Society, No. 126. John Roque's map.

The A-Z of Regency London. Introduction by Paul Laxton [Harry Margary, Lympne Castle. Horwood's map of 1813,

The A-Z of Victorian London. Introductory notes by Ralph Hyde Harry Margary, Lympne Castle. Reproduction of G. W. Bacon's *Atlas of London 1888.*

The Times London History Atlas, ed. by Hugh Clout, Times Books

Printed Maps of Victorian London 1851-1900, by Ralph Hyde, Dawson, Folkestone

Registration Districts in England and Wales 1837-1851 and 1852-1946 (Maps), Institute of Heraldic & Genealogical Studies

Local history societies (most produce publications):

Abney Park Cemetery Trust; Acton History Group; Barking & District Historical Society; Barnet Local History Society; Barnes & Mortlake Historical Society; Bexley Historical Society; Blackheath Society; Brentford & Chiswick Local History Society; Brixton Society; Bromley Borough Local History Society; Camberwell Society; Camden History Society; Charlton Society; Chingford Historical Society; City of

London Historical Society; Clapham Society; Croydon Society; Croydon Oral History Society; Dulwich Society; Ealing Museum Art & History Society; East London History Society; Edmonton Hundred Historical Society; Edmonton Hundred Historical Society Jewish Group; Eltham Society; Enfield Archaeological Society; Enfield Preservation Society; Finchley Society; Fulham & Hammersmith Historical Society; Greenwich Historical Society; Greenwich Industrial History Society; Hackney Archives Department; Friends of Hackney Archives; Hackney Society; Heath & Old Hampstead Society; Hendon & District Archaeological Society; Holborn Society; Hornsey Historical Society; Hounslow & District Local History Society; Ilford Historical Society; Islington Archaeology and History Society; Islington Society; Lewisham Local History Society; London & Middlesex Archaeological Society; London Record Society; London Topographical Society; Merton Historical Society; Mill Hill Historical Society; Newham Historical Society; Norwood Society; Pinner Local History Society; Northwood & Eastcote Local History Society; Romford & District Historical Society; Paddington Society; Rotherhithe & Bermondsey Local History Society; St Marylebone Society; Shepherds Bush Local History Society; Shooters Hill History Group; Soho Society; Southall Local History Society; Southwark & Lambeth Archaeological Society; Stanmore & Harrow Local History Society; Thorney Island Society; The Borough of Twickenham Local History Society; Uxbridge Local History and Archives Society; Waltham Forest Civic Society; Walthamstow Historical Society; Wandsworth Historical Society; Wanstead Historical Society; Wembley History Society; Westminster Society; Willesden Local History Society; Wimbledon Society; Woodford Historical Society; Woolwich & District Antiquarian Society.

The current contact addresses of the above societies can be obtained from the relevant local record office listed in *London Local Archives.*

Many London local books are published by Messrs Sutton Publishing, Phillimore Publications, Pitkin Colour Guides, Shire Books Publications and Tempus Publishing.

USEFUL ADDRESSES

Achievements Ltd., Northgate, Canterbury, Kent CT1 IBA

Bishopsgate Institute, 230 Bishopsgate, London EC2M 4QH

BT Archives, Third floor, Holborn Telephone Exchange, 268-270 High Holborn, London WC1V 7EE

Church of England Record Centre, 15 Galleywall Road, South Bermondsey, London SE16 3PB

Corporation of London Records Office, PO Box 270 Guildhall, London EC2P 2EJ

Guildhall Library, Manuscripts Section, Aldermanbury, London EC2P 2EJ

Guildhall Library, Print Room, Aldermanbury, London EC2P 2EJ

House of Lords Record Office, House of Lords, London SWIA 0PW

London Metropolitan Archives, 40 Northampton Road, London EC1R 0HB

London Transport Archives, 55 Broadway, London SWIH 0BD

Museum of London, Library, 150 London Wall, London EC2Y 5HN

Museum of London, Docklands Project, Unit C 14, Poplar Business Park, 10 Prestons Road, London E14 9RL

Public Record Office, Ruskin Avenue, Kew, Surrey TW9 4DU

Society of Genealogists, 14 Charterhouse Buildings, Goswell Road, London ECIM 7BA

Surrey History Centre, 130 Goldsworth Road, Woking, Surrey GU21 IND

The City of Westminster Archives Centre, 10 St Ann's Street, London SWIP 2DE

'London' Family History Societies: An up-to-date list of society contacts is published in each issue of the FFHS's *Family History News and Digest.* They may be subject to change. Details of current family history society contacts may be had from **The Administrator, Federation of Family History Societies, PO Box** 2425, Coventry CV5 6YX, UK.

    East of London Family History Society

    East Surrey Family History Society

    Hillingdon Family History Society

    London & North Middlesex Family History Society

    West Middlesex Family History Society

    Westminster & Central Middlesex Family History Society

    Waltham Forest Family History Society

    North West Kent Family History Society